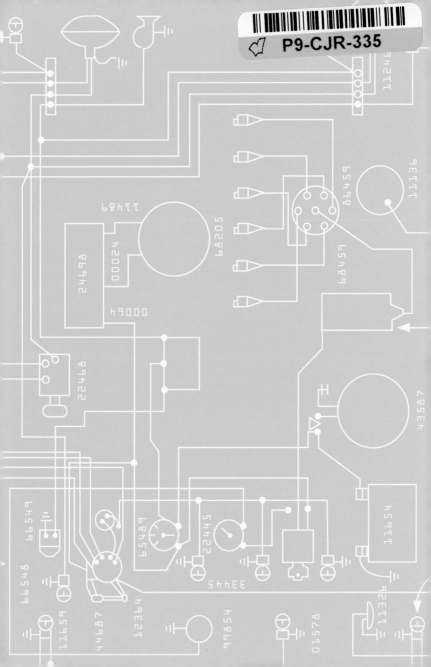

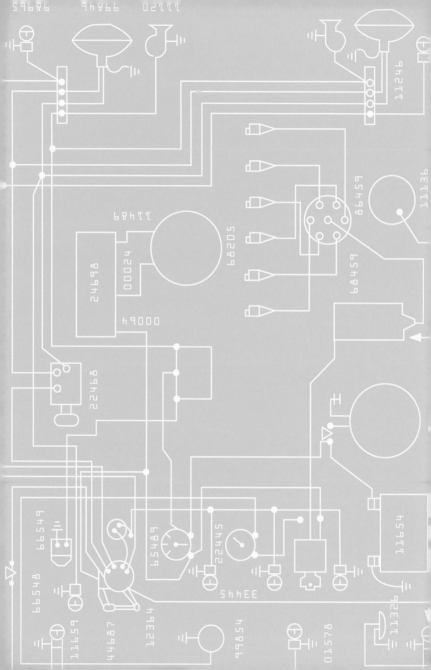

NICK AND TESLA'S

SOLAR-POWERED
SHOWDOWN

NICK AND TESLA'S

SOLAR-POWERED SHOWDOWN

A MYSTERY WITH

SUN-POWERED GADGETS YOU CAN MAKE YOURSELF

BY "SCIENCE BOB" PFLUGFELDER AND STEVE HOCKENSMITH

QUIRK BOOKS
PHILADELPHIA

ILLUSTRATIONS BY

SCOTT GARRETT

Library of Congress Cataloging in Publication Number:
2015946943

ISBN: 978-1-59474-866-0

Printed in China
Typeset in Caecilia, Futura, and Russell Square

Designed by Molly Murphy, based on a design by Doogie Horner
Illustrations by Scott Garrett
Production management by John J. McGurk

Quirk Books
215 Church Street
Philadelphia, PA 19106
quirkbooks.com

10 9 8 7 6 5 4 3 2 1

DANGER! DANGER! DANGER! DANGER!

The first time Nikola Copernicus Holt surfed the Web by himself, he was looking for pictures of Clifford the Big Red Dog. Nikola (who would soon insist on being called "Nick") didn't know how to type. And he could barely spell "big," "red," or "dog," let alone "Clifford," which came out "kifwErt" on his first attempt. But Nikola was a precocious and tenacious boy, and after lots of hunting and pecking and googling, he found Clifford.

Unfortunately, he also found—and installed and activated—much more than that. When his twin sister, Tesla Nightingale Holt, found him, Nick was crying and pounding the keyboard because the Clifford pictures had been replaced by a dozen blinking pop-up ads that filled the screen and wouldn't go away.

"I want the funny dog!" Nick wailed.

His parents just wanted their computer to work—and it did, but only after several hours of laborious debugging to remove all the malware that Nick had unwittingly downloaded. When they were finished, the Holts told both children they were not to use the computer again without adult supervision.

Tesla started crying, because she had lost a privilege she didn't even know she had. And it was all her brother's fault and it just wasn't fair.

Nick started crying, again, because he still wanted to see the funny dog.

All this drama happened when Nick and Tesla were four and a half years old.

Over the next seven years, Nick spent many an hour on many a computer. But he never again downloaded a virus because he always remembered to be careful and cautious.

Until now.

"I say we open it," Nick announced.

He reached for the ENTER key on the laptop computer.

Tesla reached over the screen to block him.

The twins were sitting on the floor of the cramped second-floor bedroom they'd been sharing all summer in their Uncle Newt's house. They were facing each other, with the computer between them.

Nick stabbed his finger at the computer keyboard.

Tesla reached to yank the laptop away . . .

In the distance a BOOM sounded, and the whole house seemed to lift into the air around them and then slam back down.

The lights shut off. So did the laptop screen.

Nick and Tesla were too stunned to speak, which is why they were able to hear their uncle calling to them from deep in the basement of the house.

"I'm all right!" Uncle Newt shouted. "It's a surprise!"

For a moment, everything was silent. Then Tesla let out a sigh of relief. She and her brother had learned that house-shaking blasts were a common occurrence when Uncle Newt was in the basement. It was where he worked on his various inventions—

all of them prone to exploding.

"For a second I thought you'd set off some kind of booby trap," Tesla said to Nick.

"The power went off before I could hit ENTER," he replied.

Then the lights came back on.

And so did the laptop. And when the twins' eyes adjusted to the suddenly bright room, the computer screen was back on and the same words were still flashing, flashing, flashing:

OPEN THIS FILE IF YOU WANT TO SAVE YOUR PARENTS . . .
OPEN THIS FILE IF YOU WANT TO SAVE YOUR PARENTS . . .
OPEN THIS FILE IF YOU WANT TO SAVE YOUR PARENTS . . .

Nick and Tesla hadn't seen their mother and father in more than a month—not since their parents had driven them to Dulles International Airport outside Washington, D.C., and put them on a flight to San Francisco. The twins were supposed to have a fun-filled visit with their Uncle Newt in Half Moon Bay, California, while Mr. and Mrs. Holt, horticulture experts for the U.S. Department of Agriculture, traveled to the Central Asian country of Uzbekistan to study revolutionary soybean irrigation techniques.

Supposedly.

But soon after arriving in Half Moon Bay, the kids discovered that their parents were in fact working on a top-secret space-based solar-power project. *And* that they were on the run from someone who wanted to steal their discoveries. *And* that this evil someone had sent spies to capture Nick and Tesla. *And* that mysterious government agents monitoring the whole mess would occasionally come swooping in when the bad guys got too close. *And* . . . no, that's all the ands for now.

All in all, it had been one of their more eventful summers.

But Nick didn't particularly like excitement, and he was worried about his mom and dad. Which was why he had been spending so much time online, obsessively researching space-based solar power and satellites and conspiracy theories.

Then, just minutes ago, Nick had been scrolling through the forums on a particularly paranoid website for young conspiracy nuts (tinfoilhatsjr.ntz). Suddenly, *it* had appeared on the screen: a pop-up box with ten large, flashing words that said

That's when Nick's argument with Tesla began.

And it wasn't over yet.

"Let's try that again," said Nick, once more reaching for the ENTER key.

"Let's not," said Tesla, throwing her arms over the keyboard to block him.

"I can't believe you're stopping me!" Nick fumed.

"I can't believe you need to be stopped," Tesla snapped. Like most brothers and sisters, Nick and Tesla argued from time to time. But this particular argument was unusual. Typically *Tesla* was the one who wanted to do something risky and *Nick* was the one who argued against it. This time, Nick was sure that clicking on the mysterious pop-up message would lead them to important information about their missing parents. But Tesla was equally sure that it was a bad and risky idea.

They paused their squabbling for a few seconds while each of their brains adjusted to being on an unfamiliar side of the argument. Then Nick started up again: "That message is a huge clue!"

Tesla jumped in. "That message is an obvious

trap."

"You're being paranoid!"

"You're being reckless."

"Just listen to me!"

"Just listen to *me*."

"This is stupid!"

"Yes," Tesla said, "it is."

Nick threw up his hands, leaning back away from the computer. "OK, fine. You win," he grumbled.

"Good," said Tesla. "Now what we should do is . . . HEY!"

The second Tesla let her guard down, Nick stabbed at the ENTER key.

This time, instead of blocking his hand, Tesla snatched the laptop and jerked it away.

Nick tried to grab it back. "We've got to give it a try!" he said.

Tesla hopped to her feet and backed away.

Nick stood and stepped toward her. "Why won't you let me open it?"

"Because we don't know what it is."

"That's exactly why we have to open it!"

Nick took another step toward Tesla. There wasn't much space for her to maneuver—the bedroom was only a little larger than a fairly roomy closet—so she was forced to hop onto her bed. (Actually, although it had a mattress, the bed wasn't really a bed; it was a biomass thermal-conversion station. That's a bed-like thingie created by their uncle that uses the body heat of a sleeping person to turn composted kitchen scraps into energy. Uncle Newt's house was filled with all kinds of these crazy contraptions.)

"You know how dumb it is to click on random pop-ups," Tesla said.

"This isn't random! It's a message! To us! About Mom and Dad!" Nick shifted from one foot to the other, trying to decide when to make his next move.

"That's just what it *claims* to be. It's probably a trick." Tesla kept her eyes fixed on her brother, figuring that she had the advantage now that she was on higher ground.

"So what if it is?" Nick asked her. "What's the worst that could happen?"

"We ruin one of Uncle Newt's computers."

"That's a small price to pay!"

"Easy for you to say. You're not the one who'd pay it."

Nick opened his mouth to reply, but then shut it

and just growled.

"Give up?" Tesla asked. "For real this time?"

"Not quite yet," Nick said. "How much do you think it would cost to replace that laptop?"

"It doesn't matter, because we're not going to ruin it."

"Just answer me. How much?"

"Well . . ." As she often did when running numbers in her head, Tesla rolled her eyes up and looked at the ceiling.

Which was just what Nick was waiting for. He bounded onto Tesla's "bed" and snatched away the laptop with a gleeful "Yoink!"

"Hey!" Tesla cried as Nick leapt to the floor and tore out of the room. She jumped down and sprinted into the hallway after him. But Nick had all the head start he needed.

Tesla caught up just in time to have the bathroom door slammed in her face. She reached out and grabbed the doorknob, but it was already locked.

"Don't click on it, Nick!" she yelled, pounding on the door.

"Can't hear you!" Nick called back in a sing-songy voice. "Too busy clicking!"

Tesla stopped banging on the door, and a moment passed in silence. Then she heard her brother groan.

"Aww, man," he said.

"What happened?"

"It *was* a trick. But not the kind you thought it was."

"What do you mean?"

Tesla heard the door unlock. Nick pulled it open and stepped into the hall to show her the computer screen.

The pop-up box was still there, but to the original message of

OPEN THIS FILE IF YOU WANT TO SAVE YOUR PARENTS . . .

new words had been added:

UP TO 30% ON THEIR CAR INSURANCE!

Below the flashing headline was a bunch of fine print and what looked like an application, along with a picture of a bland couple grinning at their equally bland kids. Because, presumably, they were now saving up to 30 percent on their car insurance.

Nick closed the laptop and handed it to Tesla, trudging back to their bedroom.

"We'll be with Mom and Dad again, just wait and see," Tesla said as he passed. "We just have to be patient."

"I don't want to wait and see. I don't want to be patient anymore," Nick said. "I want to go find them." Then Tesla heard Nick flop onto his biomass thermal-conversion station. (Yes, he had one, too.) She followed into the bedroom and found Nick lying facedown with a pillow over his head.

Tesla set the laptop on the floor and sat beside him.

"Umuhme yuh thu wuh luhkee fuh tuhwuh," Nick said.

Tesla picked up the pillow.

"What?"

Nick lifted his head so he wasn't speaking directly into his biomass thermal-conversion station. "Usually you're the one looking for trouble," he repeated.

Tesla couldn't deny it. She had been dragging her brother into one misadventure after another ever since they arrived in Half Moon Bay. It was her way of distracting herself from her worries.

Then they heard a muffled *thump* (not as loud this time), and the whole house shook again.

Tesla was about to get up and say something like, "Come on—it's time we found out what Uncle Newt's up to." But she changed her mind and stayed by her brother.

"You're not going to find Mom and Dad on the Internet, you know," Tesla said.

"So what am I supposed to do? Nothing?"

"No. I just think we should focus on something

that could really get us some answers."

"Like what?" Nick said. He was starting to grouse but then rolled over and sat up, smiling. "Did you say 'we'?"

With the exception of a brief break for dinner—which a distracted Nick and Tesla wolfed down without even tasting—the kids spent the rest of the day pacing around their room trying to figure out where to begin their search. In the end, their analysis boiled down to this:

Should they go back to the last place they'd seen their parents—Washington, D.C.?

No, that would be pointless. Their parents had gone into hiding after seeing them off at the airport.

Should they try to track their parents down through the United States Department of Agriculture?

No. Nick and Tesla had realized over the past few weeks that their parents had never really worked for the USDA. That was just a cover story.

Should they hire a detective?

No. Too expensive. Anyway, would a private eye take orders from a couple of eleven-year-olds?

Should they contact Agent McIntyre, the government operative who had been keeping an eye on them since they arrived in Half Moon Bay?

No. Because—no, wait! Yes! Yes, that was it!

"She definitely knows more than she's let on about where Mom and Dad have gone and who's after them," Tesla said. "If we want answers, we should start with Agent McIntyre."

"But how do we get in touch with her?" Nick asked.

"There's always these." Tesla pulled at a thin chain around her neck. Hanging from it was a small gold star.

Nick wore an identical chain and star. Agent McIntyre had given them the pendants, telling the twins to "wear them close to their hearts."[1] Nick and Tesla assumed they were tracking devices of some sort, but they didn't know how they worked.

Not for the first time, Nick pulled out his gold

1 Spoiler alert! This happened at the end of Nick and Tesla's Secret Agent Gadget Battle.—The authors

star and shouted into it.

"Hel-loooooo! Agent McIntyre! Nick Holt calling! Would you mind popping by to explain what the heck's been going on this summer?"

He waited for a moment and then stuffed the pendant back under his shirt.

"Nothing," he said. "Like always."

"Well, there's got to be some way we can use them to get her attention," Tesla said, glaring down at her own pendant. "Otherwise, what's the point of these things?"

Nick gave his sister a thoughtful look . . . which was interrupted by a huge, loud yawn from somewhere downstairs.

Tesla glanced at the clock and then turned, heading for the bedroom door.

"Come on. It's time to tuck in Uncle Newt."

Nick and Tesla's uncle tended to fall asleep slumped over one of the worktables in his basement laboratory. He did it so often that the kids had gotten into the habit of going downstairs every night at ten o'clock to wake him up and send him to bed.

"Can you do it by yourself tonight?" Nick said. He stretched out on his thermal-conversion station, put his hands under his head, and stared up at the ceiling. "I want to keep thinking."

"Sure. Be right back."

Tesla went down to the first floor and walked past the bric-a-brac lining the hall (dust-covered computers, an old-fashioned diving suit, a Christmas tree decorated with stained and broken beakers, and on and on). When she reached the kitchen at the back of the house, she headed down the rickety steps to the basement.

"Uncle Newt!" she called.

"What? Who? When? Where? Why?" she heard her uncle mutter groggily.

"It's ten o'clock," Tesla said. "Time to come upstairs and—"

"Hold it right there!" Uncle Newt cried out.

Tesla stopped. She had almost reached the bottom of the steps, and she could see the soot-covered machines and scorched electronic components and half-finished inventions that filled her uncle's poorly lit lab (an accordion-powered hair dryer, spray-on galoshes, the remains of a kind of goo that once glued Uncle Newt to the floor, and on and on).

Her uncle was stumbling around one of the

clutter-covered worktables, obviously hurrying to put himself between it and Tesla. He had one hand tucked behind his back, like a five-year-old trying to hide the cookie he'd just fished from the cookie jar. He was wearing his usual stained lab coat over his usual ratty T-shirt. Also as usual, fresh smoke was swirling around his wild, graying hair.

"I'm working on a surprise, remember?" Uncle Newt said. "Surprises aren't surprising if you've seen them in advance."

"Oh. Right. Sorry. I just wanted to tell you that it's ten o'clock. Time to go upstairs and brush your teeth."

Uncle Newt relaxed a bit but didn't take his hand from behind his back.

"Thanks, Tesla. I think I might stay up a little later tonight, actually. CNN's about to show a special on the new Treaty on Principles Governing the Activities of States in the Exploration and Use of Outer Space, including the Moon and Other Celestial Bodies."

"You mean the international space weapons ban?" said Tesla.

Tesla and Nick had always been fascinated

by space science—all kinds of science, really, but space science especially. So a new treaty outlawing weapons platforms outside the Earth's atmosphere wasn't something that would escape their notice. Under normal circumstances, they would be begging their parents to let them stay up to watch a TV special on the subject.

"Exactly," Uncle Newt said. And with his free hand he waved a wisp of smoke from in front of his face. "They're going to discuss how the Treaty on Principles Governing the Activities of States in the Exploration—"

"You don't have to say it again, Uncle Newt. I know what it's called."

"Right. Well, they're going to discuss how the new version of the treaty is different from the one we signed back in the nineteen-sixties. The show comes on at ten-thirty. Would you and Nick like to watch it with me? We could pop corn. I don't have any real popcorn, but there's a can of Niblets that might do interesting things if we dumped it into a pot of hot oil."

"No, thanks. Nick and I are . . . doing something else."

"All right, then. I'll tell you everything they got wrong in the morning. Good night."

"Good night," said Tesla.

As she left the basement, Uncle Newt pivoted stiffly to keep whatever was behind his back out of her line of sight.

"Any brainstorms while I was gone?" she asked her brother as she walked back into their bedroom.

There was no answer.

Nick was fast asleep.

Tesla's mother and father were talking to her, saying something that seemed to worry them, but she couldn't hear their words.

"What?" Tesla said.

Her parents began shouting, looking alarmed, yet still Tesla heard nothing.

"What?" she repeated. "What is it? What are you trying to tell me?"

Her mother and father screamed silently. And then, at last, Tesla heard a sound.

Footsteps. By her bed.

She woke up.

Tesla opened one eye and saw the ghostly gray light of early morning.

A dark figure was standing near her feet, holding something big and bulky that made an ominous sizzling noise.

Tesla shot out from under the covers and raised her fists.

"Back off!" she said. "I know kung fu!"

The dark figure laughed. Only it wasn't a dark figure anymore, because now both of Tesla's eyes were wide open.

It was Nick. He was wearing a black T-shirt and a red swimsuit and he was holding a large plate. On the plate was a meat thermometer, two forks, and a half-eaten ham Uncle Newt's girlfriend Hiroko had made for them two nights ago.

It was the ham that was sizzling.

"Sorry to scare you like that, but I just couldn't wait to get started," Nick said.

Tesla blinked at the ham, wondering if she was still dreaming.

"Get started with what?"

Nick grinned. "I have a plan," he said.

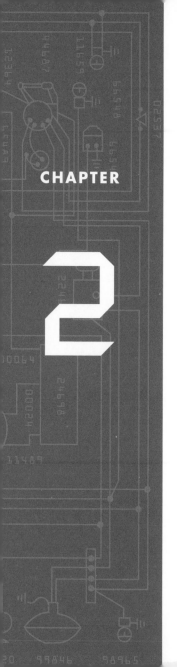

Nick didn't explain his plan. He simply said, "Put on your bathing suit and meet me out front." Then he turned and walked out of the room.

He assumed that Tesla would work it all out by the time she was dressed. A warm ham, a meat thermometer, forks, swimsuits—the plan was obvious, wasn't it?

Nick waited on the sidewalk in front of Uncle Newt's house, watching the sun rise over the tall forested hills to the east of Half Moon Bay. After only a few minutes Tesla poked her head out the front door, looked him over, and said,

"Why didn't you grab some towels?"

"Because I forgot we'd need them."

Tesla rolled her eyes and went back inside.

Nick had assumed correctly . . . the plan was obvious. At least to his sister.

Tesla returned with two mismatched towels—finding *anything* that matched in Uncle Newt's house was a challenge—and then she and Nick set off down the street, heading west.

Tesla looked at the gold star dangling from its chain above the top of her swimsuit. "So you think these things aren't just tracking devices," she said to Nick. "They might be monitoring our environment and vital signs, too."

Nick nodded. "You reminded me last night: Agent McIntyre told us to wear them close to our hearts.[2] I'd assumed she was being sentimental or something. But then I started thinking . . . maybe

---

2   That was at the end of *Nick and Tesla's Secret Agent Gadget Battle*, remember? Like we told you in the last footnote?
    —The authors

that wasn't it at all. Maybe she wanted to watch our heart rates."

Tesla pointed at the meat thermometer, which was jammed deep into the ham that Nick was carrying. "And our body temperatures?"

"Exactly. I nuked the ham pretty good in the microwave. The internal temperature's around . . ." Nick tilted his head to get a good look at the meat thermometer's red needle. ". . . one hundred eighty degrees. But it's dropping fast."

"Of course it is. The ham's small, so it has a high surface-area-to-volume ratio," said Tesla.

"Right. That means it's going to cool off a lot more quickly than we would," said Nick. "If we, you know, stopped producing body heat."

"And heartbeats."

"Exactly." Nick rechecked the thermometer. "So we'll provide a reason for the quick drop in our core temperature and the no-heartbeat thing."

"It's a pretty mean trick, actually," Tesla noted. "Making Agent McIntyre think we might be bobbing around in the ocean, dead."

"I know it is. But can you think of another way to start looking for Mom and Dad?"

"I'm here, aren't I?" said Tesla. She didn't like to admit when she couldn't think of something, so that was her way of saying "No."

Then, at the same time, Tesla and Nick both stopped walking.

Up to that point in their sunrise stroll, Uncle Newt's street looked like a lot of northern California neighborhoods. They had passed small yards, medium houses, big trees. But the end of this particular street was something special.

The slow, steady rhythm of pounding surf had been growing louder as the twins headed west, and now it was impossible to ignore. Seagulls soared overhead. The salty, pungent scent of the sea was overwhelming.

Nick and Tesla had reached a ridge overlooking Half Moon Bay State Beach and, beyond it, the Pacific Ocean. Even in the dim light of dawn—which, of course, was concentrated in the east, behind them—the horizon before them was vast. They could see nothing but a strip of sand and rocks stretching into the impossible distance. Straight ahead, gray waves were swallowing all the world.

A narrow trail in the steep, scrub-covered hill

zigzagged down to the beach about eighty feet below. Tesla started down and didn't look back. Crazy
as Nick's plan was, she knew it was their best shot.

Nick and Tesla walked just close enough to the
ocean for the surf to wash over their toes and then
they checked the ham's temperature. It was down to
one hundred fifty degrees Fahrenheit. They couldn't
put their plan into action till the thermometer reg-
istered between 97.7 and 99.5 degrees—the normal
core temperature of a human being.

Which meant the ham had to cool a bit. Tesla
sped up the process by moving farther into the
chilly water and dipping the ham in the surf while
Nick chased off the gulls that started swooping toward them when they noticed the chunk of
delicious-smelling meat. A bony, tanned old man
wearing nothing but teeny yellow running shorts,
black socks, and sneakers shot them a quizzical look
as he jogged past, but didn't stop to ask why two
kids were giving a ham a bath in the ocean.

This was California, after all.

After a few minutes of ham swishing and gull dodging, Tesla announced: "We're there! Just below one hundred degrees! Now what?"

"Maybe we should run around a little before we take off our pendants," Nick suggested. "You know—spike our heart rates so it'll look like spies are after us again."

Tesla ducked as a screeching gull narrowly missed flying into her face.

"I don't know about you," she said, "but between these crazy birds and this freezing water, my heart rate is spiking already."

"Good point. Mine too. Let's make the switch."

The twins walked out of the water and knelt by the plate they had left on the sand, next to their towels. On the plate were the two forks.

Nick grabbed a fork with one hand and his pendant with the other. "I'll go first. Give me a countdown."

"Three, two, one. Go!" Tesla said.

Nick jerked the pendant over his head and wrapped the chain around the fork's tines. Then he plunged the fork into the ham so that the pendant was speared to its pink, slimy side.

31

"Right. I'm dead," Nick said. "Your turn."

Tesla repeated the maneuver, pinning her pendant into the ham next to her brother's. If the pendants worked the way Nick and Tesla thought they did, whoever was monitoring the signal would no longer be detecting their heartbeats. But because the ham was keeping the pendants at body temperature, it would seem like they were still wearing them.

Which meant . . . well, it meant that whoever was on the other end of the signal would need to check out what was going on.

"OK," Nick said, picking up the ham. "Into the water again."

He and Tesla waded back into the ocean, holding the ham. When they were out far enough for the waves to crash up to their thighs, Nick bent down to keep the meat in the frothy, frigid water. He dared not loosen his grip because of an interesting scientific discovery the pair made: Ham sinks.

Almost immediately, both Nick and Tesla were shivering. It was hardly even waist-high, but the water was *cold*.

"How long do you think we'll need to do this?"

Tesla asked.

Nick shrugged. "Depends on how near Agent McIntyre is. And if she gets the signal. And if the pendants really are monitoring our life signs. And if—"

"OK, OK! Enough ifs!" Tesla said through chattering teeth. "You're already making me r-r-r-regret this!"

A sudden splashing sounded behind them, and the twins turned to see a huge golden retriever charging right at them, his leash dragging limply through the sea foam.

"Buttons! Buttons!" a plump middle-aged woman in a powder blue tracksuit was calling from the beach. "Come back here!"

Nick turned his back to Buttons and hugged the ham to his chest.

Tesla wasn't particularly anxious to put herself between an unfamiliar dog and a block of meat. But she didn't seem to have a choice: If Tesla didn't do *something*, and fast, Buttons the dog would get the ham and their pendants would end up in his canine stomach.

So Tesla grabbed the leash and began tugging

33

the dog toward the beach. Buttons struggled and whined at first, but eventually the food frenzy evaporated and he let Tesla lead him out of the water.

"Thank you so much," the woman said as Tesla handed her the leash. "I hope he didn't scare you. I don't know what got into him."

"Oh, that's OK," Tesla said, giving Buttons a friendly pat. She nodded at her brother, who was still standing in the ocean about thirty yards away. "He was just after our ham."

Nick gave the woman a friendly wave. The meat was now tucked under his other arm.

The woman's eyes bulged.

"Come on, Buttons," she muttered, spinning around and hurrying off without another word. With obvious reluctance, Buttons let her drag him away.

Nick bent down and again lowered the ham into the water.

"You know what I just realized?" Tesla shouted to Nick. (She had to really yell to be heard over the surf.) "There's no reason we *both* have to be out there in the freezing water."

Nick started to yell back something sarcastic, but just then a particularly persistent gull dove at him.

He frantically shooed it away.

Tesla was right. It took only one set of hands to hold the ham in the water, and this nutty idea had been Nick's. If either one of them had to get hypothermia from submerging a ham into frigid seawater, Nick decided that it should be him.

He turned toward shore and was about to yell exactly that when suddenly Tesla cried out: "Nick! Look!"

Nick's eyes went wide with fear. Tesla was pointing frantically at something behind him.

Tesla, and their mother, too, sometimes called Nick "Little Mr. Sunshine" or "Mr. Worst-Case Scenario," because he had an impressively vivid imagination, especially when it came to picturing how just about anything could go ruinously, horribly wrong. But Nick suddenly realized that he didn't even *need* a vivid imagination to know why it might not be smart to splash around holding a hunk of pink, juicy, cooked meat in ocean waters known to host the occasional great white shark. For once, Nick's instinct for predicting imminent disaster had failed him—until now, that is, when it was perhaps too late. Nick whipped around, fully expecting to see a big gray triangle of a shark's dorsal fin slicing through the water as it zoomed toward him.

Something big and sleek *was* heading Nick's way. But it wasn't slicing through the water.

The twins stared with mouths agape as a streamlined orange-and-white Coast Guard helicopter flew toward the beach. As it approached, it slowed and lost altitude. In a few more seconds it stopped, hovering about a hundred feet in front of, and above, Nick. The whirling blades made choppy ripples in the water.

The chopper hung there for a moment, its rotors roaring even louder than the surf. Louder still was a jarring crackle of static and an amplified male voice booming: "NICK AND TESLA HOLT?"

"Yes!" said Nick.

"That's us!" yelled Tesla.

Another long moment passed. Then the voice blared again:

"GO HOME!"

The helicopter swung its nose to the south and shot off, following the shoreline. In less than a minute, it was nothing but a speck in the sky.

"Well, I guess your plan kind of worked," Tesla said as she and her brother trudged up the street toward their uncle's house.

"There's no such thing as 'kind of worked,'" Nick said bitterly. "Either we got information out of Agent McIntyre or we didn't. And we didn't."

Tesla stayed silent.

As their uncle's house came into view, Nick bent forward and breathed in deeply through his nose. "Great," he grumbled. "I smell like ham. It's gonna remind me all day that we failed."

"No, it won't! Because we didn't!" Tesla said. Nick looked up.

A black SUV was parked in front of Uncle Newt's house, and two unhappy-looking people were standing next to it. One was a tall, thin man with gray hair. The other was a red-haired woman wearing a dark pantsuit and sunglasses. And a scowl.

Agent McIntyre.

"So you're alive, huh?" she said to Nick and Tesla as they approached the car. "Well, we might just have to remedy that."

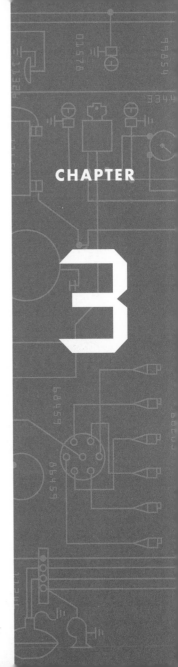

"I'm really, really sorry, Agent McIntyre. Really."

This was Nick's seventh apology (and his twenty-first "really"). He and Tesla were sitting on rusty lawn furniture on the back patio of their uncle's house, still wrapped in soggy towels. Agent McIntyre and her colleague—a taciturn man they'd met briefly once before[3]—stood stiffly nearby, glaring at the kids through identical black mir-

---

3   That was also at the end of *Nick and Tesla's Secret Agent Gadget Battle.* Hey, a lot happened in that book! Don't blame us if you haven't read it yet!—The authors

rored sunglasses.

"I know it must have freaked you out thinking we might be . . . in trouble," Nick continued. "But we couldn't figure out what else to do."

"It's not like we had a bat-signal we could use to call you," Tesla added. "How were we supposed to communicate with you?"

"You weren't," Agent McIntyre said sternly. "And now I have to explain to my bosses why I scrambled a Coast Guard helicopter to intercept a couple of kids playing on the beach with a Nerf ball."

"It wasn't a Nerf ball," Nick said. "It was a—"

"Tesla! Nick! There you are!"

Before Nick could explain any further, Uncle Newt came out of the house, holding a cardboard container a little larger than a shoe box. He was in his modern mad-scientist uniform: frayed blue jeans, T-shirt, and a white lab coat burned in several places. His hair was even more unkempt than usual (which meant that it looked like he had just stuck his finger in an electrical socket). If he was surprised to find a pair of glowering government agents on his back patio, he didn't show it. "What's going on here?" would have been the most obvious thing to ask in this situation. But Uncle Newt seldom did the obvious.

"Hey, who's up for a barbecue?" he asked instead.

A grill stood on the edge of the patio, next to the patchy lawn, and it was in about a thousand pieces. Scorch marks on the nearby concrete and grass made it clear that, like so many things around Uncle Newt's house, it had, at some point, exploded.

"Do you know what these two kids were up to this morning?" Agent McIntyre said to Uncle Newt, wagging her finger accusingly between Nick and

Tesla.

Uncle Newt looked at his damp niece and equally soggy nephew and then frowned.

"Kids, kids, kids," he said, shaking his head. "I am very disappointed. I manage to remember to tell you one responsible grown-up thing—never go swimming without an adult—and you ignore me. Consider your Twinkies privileges revoked until further notice!"

Uncle Newt put the cardboard box on a lawn chair, stepped over to Agent McIntyre and shook her hand, and then did the same to the other agent.

"Thank you for bringing them home. I'm sure it won't happen again. But, say. As long as you're here, how about sticking around for a barbecue? Wienies on me!"

"Mr. Holt," Agent McIntyre said slowly, her tone verging on exasperation.

"Doctor Holt, actually," Uncle Newt said, correcting her.

"*Doctor* Holt—"

"Or stick with Mister, if you prefer." Uncle Newt shrugged. "I'm not a medical doctor. I don't want to turn into one of those stuffed shirts who wants everyone to call him 'Doctor So-and-So' because he has a PhD in modern dance."

"All right. Mr. Holt—"

"You know what? Let's skip the formality altogether. Just call me Newt!"

By this time, Agent McIntyre's normally pale face was flushed as crimson as her strawberry-red hair.

She turned to the other agent.

"You tell him," she said between gritted teeth.

"Your niece and nephew played a cruel trick on Agent McIntyre and me," said the other agent, "resulting in the waste of our valuable time and a distraction from our important duties."

Uncle Newt cocked his head and narrowed his eyes. "They played a cruel trick on you?"

The man nodded.

"In their bathing suits?" Uncle Newt said.

"Yes."

"Look," Tesla said, interrupting, "our parents are on the run from spies—one of whom turned out to be our uncle's neighbor.[4] Didn't you think we'd try to find out what's going on?" The old lawn chair

---

4   We don't need to tell you which book that was in, do we? You
     know by now.—The authors

creaked as Tesla jumped to her feet. "If you'd just tell us the truth and check in with us from time to time," she said, glaring at the two agents, "we wouldn't have to play stupid tricks to get your attention."

Like his partner, the male agent was pale, though his skin seemed more ash gray than white. Where Agent McIntyre looked as if she didn't get enough sun, this guy looked like he'd spent the past year gathering dust in a closet.

"Agent McIntyre and I are special operatives of the United States government," he said to Tesla. "We're not going to give out our phone numbers and e-mail addresses to children."

"You could've kept in touch with me," Uncle Newt pointed out.

The man returned an icy stare. "Like I said . . . we aren't going to give out our contact information . . . to children."

Uncle Newt scratched his head. "Hey," he said, mumbling, "have I just been insulted?"

"The point is," the agent said, turning back to Tesla, "locating your parents is *our* job, and you're not making it any easier by—"

"Doyle!" Agent McIntyre snapped.

But it was too late. Agent Doyle had already said too much.

Tesla's eyes widened. Nick stood up. Even Uncle Newt, who usually looked like he was drawing blueprints in his mind when someone else was talking, stared at Agent Doyle with complete attention.

"*Locating* their parents?" Uncle Newt said. "You mean you don't even know where Al and Martha are?"

Agent McIntyre shot her partner a glare before answering. "There have been . . . setbacks over the past few weeks," she said.

"Losing my mom and dad isn't a setback!" Nick cried. "It's a disaster!"

"The last time we saw you, Julie, the spy from next door, was your prisoner," said Tesla. "You said you were closing in on the others. What happened?"

"Julie escaped," the male agent said.

Just in case anyone missed his name the first time McIntyre said it, she blurted it out again: "Doyle! SHUT! UP!"

"No, McIntyre. I won't! They need to know what we're up against."

Doyle took three steps forward so that he was

looming over Nick and Tesla.

"This isn't a game," he said to the twins. "This is serious business. *Life and death* business. You two want to help your parents? Stay out of it." And with that, Agent Doyle spun on the heels of his shiny black shoes and marched away.

"I'm sorry," Agent McIntyre said. "I don't think he should have said any of that. But Doyle's right. Just trust us and everything will turn out fine."

Agent McIntyre turned and quickly walked away, following Agent Doyle around the side of the house in the direction of the street.

As they listened to the black SUV pulling away, Nick and Tesla looked at each other. Their expressions were grim but determined, and each knew exactly what the other was thinking.

To their surprise, it was Uncle Newt who said it aloud.

"'Just trust us'?" he sputtered. "Trust the people who lost your parents and let one of the bad guys escape? I don't think so."

"So we're *not* staying out of it?" Nick asked.

Uncle Newt shook his head.

"You two have taught me a lot this summer," he

said. "The importance of getting involved to solve problems. The power of friendship and collaboration. How to make a grilled cheese sandwich. So, no. When I hear that my brother and his wife—your mother and father—are missing, that maybe they've been kidnapped by some sort of spy ring, I am *not* going to stay out of it." Uncle Newt paused and caught his breath. "I'm going to get into it!" he said. "I'm going to get into it all the way up to my neck! And you can get in with me if you want."

The speech wasn't quite as inspiring as Uncle Newt seemed to think it was, but Nick and Tesla appreciated the sentiment all the same.

"Thanks, Uncle Newt," said Nick.

"So, what's the plan?" asked Tesla.

Uncle Newt beamed at them with an expression that said he knew exactly where to start. "First," he declared, "we're going to have lunch!"

"Lunch?" said Nick.

"Or breakfast, I guess. It's still early. Whatever, don't split hairs. We're gonna eat!" Uncle Newt retrieved the cardboard box that he had set down earlier, opened it, and pulled out a red tube about a foot long.

47

"Behold!" Uncle Newt said, using the "science reveal" voice he favored when unleashing a new invention. "The creation I've been perfecting just for you! A *solar-powered hot dog cooker!*"

Nick and Tesla gaped at the little canister their uncle was holding.

"*That's* what you've been working on in the basement all these weeks?" asked Tesla, after about thirty seconds of gaping.

Uncle Newt nodded proudly.

"Then what's been blowing up?" asked Nick. "That thing looks like it's made out of an old Pringles can."

"That's the beauty of it! It is!" said Uncle Newt. "The early prototypes were a bit more ambitious. And big. I tried to boost the photovoltaic energy by surrounding the cooking chamber with alkane gases."

"Huh?" said Nick.

Nick loved science, but chemistry wasn't his forte.

"He was pumping them full of methane," Tesla explained.

"Mostly propane, actually. And butane a few

times," Uncle Newt said, correcting his niece. He sighed wistfully. "But the result was always the same."

"Boom?" Nick guessed.

Uncle Newt nodded. "I guess it was for the best," he said. "I was only trying to build a sun oven because you two had become so interested in solar energy. So souping it up with gas was kind of missing the point. I wanted to end up with something bigger than a hot dog cooker, though. I was going to bake an entire ham with heat energy from the sun! But then, like you say—*boom!*—so I asked Hiroko to bake it for us instead. The last time I tried to cook—"

"We remember," Nick said. The local fire department probably remembered, too. It's not often an entire company of firefighters is required to extinguish a pan of brownies.

"Speaking of ham," said Uncle Newt, "have either of you seen it? I could've sworn we still had half of it in the fridge—"

"Show us how the hot dog cooker works, Uncle Newt!" Tesla blurted out.

"Yeah, I'm starving!" Nick said. "A hot dog would really hit the spot."

Uncle Newt grinned and began searching for the perfect place to operate the solar cooker.

Nick and Tesla looked at each other with relief. Neither one felt like explaining what had happened to the ham.

"Here's a nice sunny spot," Uncle Newt said after a few minutes of wandering around the yard. He knelt and positioned the cooker just so on a far corner of the patio. "Before you know it, we'll have delicious cooked hot dogs and then we'll be ready to get to work. After all . . ."

He stood up and rubbed his hands together.

"You can't bust an international spy ring on an empty stomach!"

GUARANTEED-NOT-TO-EXPLODE FRANKFURTER HEATER-UPPER

THE STUFF

- A Pringles-style potato chip tube
- An uncooked hot dog
- A 12-inch bamboo skewer
- Clear tape
- Plastic wrap
- Scrap cardboard
- Scissors

- A small magnet (optional)
- A hobby knife
- A drill
- A hot-glue gun
- A responsible adult (to assist with the hobby knife, drill, and hot-glue gun)

THE SETUP

1. Have a party and eat all the potato chips! Then ask an adult to drill a hole in the center of the metal bottom of the can that is just large enough for the skewer to fit into. Then use the skewer to poke a hole in the center of the can's cap.

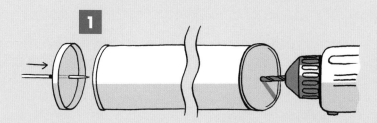

2. Don't let the responsible adult leave! You'll need help making three cuts in the can with the hobby knife, as shown in the diagram. Then open the flaps.

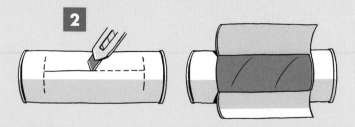

3. Cut the scrap cardboard into three pieces: one large 12-by-4-inch piece (30.5 cm by 10 cm), and two small 5-by-4-inch pieces (12.5 cm by 10 cm). Before the adult makes the cuts, be sure to check that the large piece is longer than the potato chip can. Use the skewer to poke a hole in each of the smaller pieces, along the center line of the cardboard about 2 inches (5 cm) from the end (measuring the cardboard lengthwise).

3

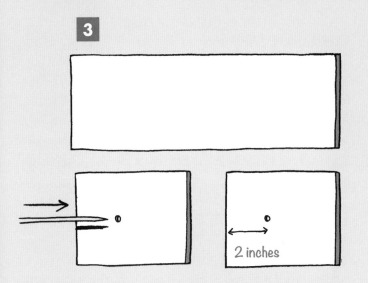

2 inches

4. Assemble the base of the heater-upper by hot-gluing the two short cardboard pieces upright on the ends of the large piece, as shown. Space the short pieces just a bit father apart than the length of the can. Place them with the holes closer to the top than the bottom.

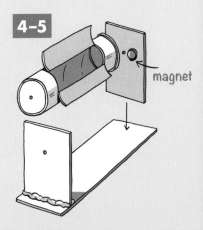

4-5

magnet

5. If you have a magnet, hot-glue it onto one of the upright cardboard pieces; place it on the inside, near the hole. It will hold the bottom of the can in place. Now you're ready to cook!

THE FINAL STEPS

1. Place the lid on the can. Holding the hot dog inside the can, carefully slip the skewer through the hole in the lid, and then through the length of the hot dog. Push the skewer carefully until it comes through the other end of the hot dog and out the hole in the bottom of the can. Center the hot dog in the can.

2. Cut a piece of plastic wrap slightly bigger than the window that your adult assistant cut into the can. Tape one end of the plastic wrap to the can, and then stretch the rest tight across the opening; tape it in place. This will trap the sun's heat in the can to cook the hot dog.

3. Place your heater-upper in a sunny spot, positioning the plastic window in direct sunlight. Adjust the position as needed to keep the hot dog facing the sun. A single hot dog will take 15 to 30 minutes to cook on a bright sunny day. It may take longer, depending on the air temperature, cloud cover, and time of day.

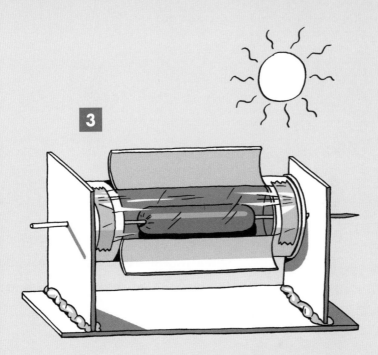

4. Once the hot dog appears cooked, remove the plastic wrap and carefully remove it from the skewer. Then stick that dog on a bun and eat up!

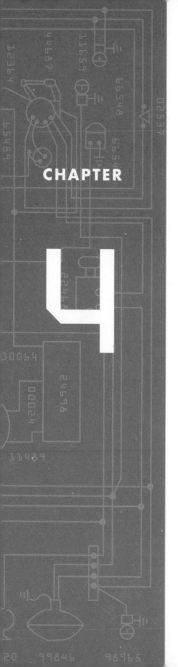

CHAPTER

4

By the time the first hot dog was ready to eat, Nick and Tesla had changed into dry clothes and built their own heater-uppers using spare parts from the lab. ("No wonder Uncle Newt's been eating so many Pringles lately," Nick said, realization dawning.) Uncle Newt graciously offered to eat the first hot dog so that his niece and nephew wouldn't argue over it.

"We could just split it," Nick suggested.

But Uncle Newt couldn't hear his nephew over the sound of his own, rather loud chewing.

"Now," Uncle Newt said, wiping at the mustard from one side of his mouth (and smearing it all over his chin), "it's time to figure out our first move."

But before they could make any plans, a voice called out from the side of the house: "Hey! You're having a barbecue and you didn't invite us?"

The person yelling was a tall, burly boy with long, curly hair—Nick and Tesla's friend Silas. With him, as usual, was his polar opposite—a slender kid with hair shaved so short, he almost looked bald: their other friend DeMarco.

"You could smell hot dogs all the way over at your house?" Tesla asked as the boys joined them on the patio.

"It wasn't the hot dogs that brought us here," said DeMarco. "It was this."

He held up a newspaper. It was the morning edition of the *San Francisco Chronicle*.

Uncle Newt squinted at the front page.

"The Giants lost again?" he sighed. "That *is* a bummer."

"I don't think that's the story that caught their eye," said Tesla.

She was looking at another headline running

across the front page. In large, blocky black letters it read:

PRESIDENT TO SIGN NEW "STAR WARS" BAN

"Don't worry, guys," Nick said. "'Star Wars' is slang for space-based weapons. That's what they're banning, not the *Star Wars* movies."

"I know that," Silas snorted. He scowled and crossed his arms over his chest, effectively covering the *Star Wars: The Force Awakens* logo on his T-shirt.

"Well, you did after we read the article," said De-Marco.

"OK, yes. I admit that I was a little freaked out at first," Silas said. "Some people really hate the prequels, you know. A ban could happen! But then, once me and DeMarco realized what was *really* being banned, we thought of your mom and dad. You guys think they're working on some kind of space laser thing, right?"

"Not exactly," said Tesla. "Space-based solar power. Satellites that collect energy from the sun and beam it to Earth as microwaves."

Silas squinted warily at the sky, as though he

half-expected a red ray to shoot down through the clouds and fry him on the spot. "Sounds like a weapon to me," he said.

"Couldn't there be a connection between what's happening with your parents and the treaty?" DeMarco asked.

Nick and Tesla looked at each other, their brows furrowed.

"Could there be?" Nick said.

"I don't see how," said Tesla. "Mom and Dad would never build something that could hurt people."

"Not on purpose, Tez," said Nick. "But what if someone was trying to take their solar-power satellite and turn it into exactly the kind of weapon the treaty would ban? Maybe that's why Mom and Dad were kidnapped."

Silas and DeMarco's eyes widened.

"*Kidnapped?*" they said together, gasping.

"Now, now. Let's not jump to conclusions," said Uncle Newt. "All we know is that Nick and Tesla's mother and father mysteriously disappeared right after one of the spies who'd been after them escaped from . . ."

Uncle Newt stopped and scratched his head.

"Never mind," he said. "They've been kidnapped."

"How do you know all this?" DeMarco asked.

Nick told them what they'd learned that morning from Agent McIntyre and Agent Doyle. When he finished, Silas shot a look at the house next door—the one that had been, for a time, the home of Julie Casserly. Uncle Newt's neighbor, and a spy. "And to think I used to mow her lawn," Silas said.

DeMarco placed a comforting hand on his friend's broad shoulder. "At least you were terrible at it."

Silas nodded, looking grimly satisfied. "Yes. Yes, I was."

He suddenly stopped, midnod. "Hey," Silas said, "someone's inside Mrs. Casserly's house right now!" He squinted and then added, "And she's watching us!"

Everyone spun around.

Silas was right. A woman was staring at them through one of the windows on the first floor of the what used to be Julie Casserly's house. She had long, straight, platinum-blonde hair and high cheekbones that were powdered pink with a heavy layer of blush. The window woman looked none too pleased by what she was seeing. Almost as soon as Nick and Tesla and everyone else got a look at her, she darted out of sight.

"Another spy!" said DeMarco.

"Or another secret agent," said Silas.

DeMarco glared at him. "Spies and secret agents are the same thing."

"No, they're not."

"Yes, they are."

"Agent McIntyre isn't a spy," Silas insisted. "She's an agent."

"But if she were a *secret* agent, she'd be a spy," DeMarco shot back.

Silas shook his head. "No. She just wouldn't call herself Agent McIntyre."

"Actually, that woman over there isn't a spy or an agent," Uncle Newt said, interrupting the boys' banter before Tesla could tell them to knock it off (one more second of debate and she would have). "She's a realtor who's been trying to sell Julie's house," Uncle Newt explained. "I've seen her bringing people by to look at it. I tried to introduce myself a few times, but I always seem to catch her at the wrong moment. Every time I go over to say hi, turns out she's late for a showing at another house."

Uncle Newt stuffed the last third of his hot dog into his mouth, smearing ketchup over the mustard already plastering his cheeks. "Iss 'oo 'ad," he said with his mouth full. He swallowed, gulping loudly, and added, "I never get to welcome her clients to the neighborhood."

That's just how the realtor wants it, Tesla thought but didn't say aloud. Instead, she said: "This might be our chance."

"You want to go welcome people to the neighborhood?" Silas asked, looking confused.

"No. I want Uncle Newt to go welcome people to the neighborhood while we—"

"Search Julie Casserly's house!" Nick said. "Great idea, Tez!"

Uncle Newt looked dubious. "Uhh . . . it is?"

"Absolutely," Nick said. "She might have left some kind of clue behind in the house. Something that could lead us to her. This is our chance to look for it, while the place is unlocked"

"But we'll need you to distract the realtor and whoever she's with," Tesla said to her uncle.

Uncle Newt thought it over for a moment and then nodded. "All right, you've come to the right man. If it's a diversion you need, a diversion you shall get. Distraction is my middle . . . hey, look at that!" Uncle Newt pointed at a small gray bird with bright patches that had landed in the branches of a nearby tree. "A yellow-rumped warbler!" he shouted. "I haven't spotted one of those in weeks. Has anyone seen my binoculars?"

Tesla snapped her fingers in front of her uncle's eyes. "Focus, Uncle Newt. You've got a job to do."

Silas started marching toward the house next door. "And so do we!"

"So, what are we looking for, anyway?" Silas whispered a few minutes later.

Nick shrugged. "A clue," he whispered back.

Silas looked around. "I don't think we're going to find one here."

Nick, Tesla, Silas, and DeMarco had managed to scramble through the front door and up the stairs while Uncle Newt cornered the realtor and her clients in the garage, introduced himself, and started talking about earthquake insurance and why anyone moving to Half Moon Bay would need plenty of it. ("Of course, it's not cheap," they could hear him saying, "but it's just a matter of time before the Big One hits and half the town ends up in the Pacific. . . . So, where are you folks from?")

While Uncle Newt prattled on, the kids darted from one room to another. But bedroom, bathroom, or closet, it didn't matter—the place was the exact opposite of Uncle Newt's house: sunny, clean, and uncluttered, and with no traces of explosions.

The house was much more than uncluttered. It was utterly, entirely empty. No beds, no dressers, no desks, no chairs, no pictures on the walls, no stains on the carpet. Not so much as a dust bunny in the corner.

With so little to search, the kids needed only a few minutes to give the upstairs a thorough once-over. They soon reconvened in the hallway, empty-handed. "Let's try downstairs," Tesla said.

She led the boys slowly down the steps, listening for any sign that the realtor was about to escape from Uncle Newt and reenter the house.

NICK AND TESLA'S SOLAR-POWERED SHOWDOWN

". . . but the wind was so strong, the dang turbine came loose, detached from the gear box, and flew right into Julie's car. Nearly split the thing in two," Uncle Newt was saying with a chuckle. "That was the last time I tried building a wind-power tower in my own backyard, let me tell you! Oh, how Julie and I laughed and laughed."

His reminiscence was followed by a moment of silence.

"Oh, wait. No, we didn't laugh," Uncle Newt said. "She threw a garden gnome at me."

The kids, meanwhile, were zigzagging around the first floor of the house. They checked the living room, kitchen, pantry, two bathrooms, and three closets. They all found the same thing.

"Nothing," Tesla reported when the group reconvened in the living room.

"Zip," said Nick.

"Zilch," said DeMarco.

"Nacho," said Silas.

His friends stared at him.

"I mean *nada*," he said. "Sorry. I'm getting hungry."

DeMarco turned to Tesla—she was usually the

65

one with a plan. "What now?" he asked.

"Maybe," Tesla began, "we—"

"Wait," Nick said, interrupting. "Do you hear something?"

Silas cocked his head and listened. "Nope," he said. "Not a thing. Why?"

Everyone else's eyes widened.

Uncle Newt wasn't talking anymore.

And someone was standing behind them. She cleared her throat.

The kids turned to find the blonde realtor glaring at them from the hallway leading to the garage. Behind her stood a much younger man and a woman. The couple looked *very* confused.

"What are you doing in here?" the realtor said with a snarl.

"Who? Us?" Tesla said. "We're just . . . uhhh . . ."

"Selling homemade hot dogs," said Nick.

The couple looked even more confused. "Homemade hot dogs?" said the man.

"Sure," Nick replied. "Some kids sell lemonade on the sidewalk. We sell hot dogs door to door. They're cooked by the heat of the sun, so they're environmentally friendly. Shall we put you down for an order of three?"

"Umm . . ." said the young woman.

"Well . . ." said the young man.

"No," said the realtor.

Nick backed toward the front door. The other kids followed suit.

"I guess we'll be on our way, then," Nick said. "Come find us if you change your minds. We'll be working this block all day. Just two dollars a dog, condiments included. Remember: if it wasn't cooked by the sun, it doesn't belong on a bun. Bye!"

By this time, Nick and the others had reached the door. All together, they spun on their heels and stampeded out.

"Let me show you a house in a *different* neighborhood," they heard the realtor saying as they left.

"How about a different *town*?" the young woman replied.

The kids retreated quickly across the lawn, headed in the direction of Uncle Newt's house.

"Think that realtor lady's gonna call the cops on us?" DeMarco asked.

"Not while there's still a chance she can sell those people a house," Nick said, adding, "I hope."

"Well, that was a complete bust," Tesla grumbled. "We didn't accomplish a thing."

"Rule for scientists number 1: Don't jump to conclusions," Uncle Newt said. He was waiting for the kids on his back porch; stretched out on a rickety lawn chair, he was holding yet another hot dog.

"What do you mean?" DeMarco asked him.

"I mean, I got a chance to talk to that realtor alone for a few seconds, while she was showing me off the property," Uncle Newt said. "And she promised to answer a question if *I* promised never to speak to her again."

"What did you ask her?" said Silas.

Uncle Newt cocked an eyebrow at his niece and nephew, challenging them to answer before he did.

"What would a realtor know about a spy?" Tesla mused.

"Nothing," said Nick. "All she would know about would be—"

Tesla blurted out the words at the same time as her brother. "The house!"

Uncle Newt nodded with satisfaction and took a big bite of his hot dog.

"Thpeifically, thu ownuhth reah namuh," he said.

"Don't talk with your mouth full," Tesla said, admonishing her uncle.

"Thorry."

Uncle Newt swallowed and then repeated his comment.

"Specifically, the owner's *real* name. That house doesn't belong to Julie Casserly, kids. It was bought for her by someone named Louis Quatorze."

"Louis Squatorzi? What the heck kind of name is that?" Silas said.

"A rare one," said Tesla. "Which is good news."

"Why would that be good news?" DeMarco asked.

Nick was nodding. He understood immediately.

"Because," he said, "that's going to make it a lot easier for us to find the guy."

5

The friends began their search where nearly every twenty-first-century investigation begins. Where even Sherlock Holmes would have begun, if he'd had the option.

Google.

Uncle Newt did the googling at the dining room table in his dusty, disorderly house. As he typed on his laptop, the kids peered at the screen over his bony shoulders.

Within seconds, Google had found three Louis Quatorzes.

The first was a French manufacturer of designer handbags.

The second was a racehorse.

The third was Louis XIV, king of France from 1643 to 1715. (*Quatorze*, it turned out, is French for "fourteen.")

"Well, that makes it easy," DeMarco said. "Obviously the handbag people are behind everything."

Tesla scowled at him. "You think my parents were kidnapped by a company that makes purses?"

"You think your parents were kidnapped by a racehorse or a dead king?" DeMarco shot back.

"Touché, DePolo," said Uncle Newt. (Though he could rattle off the entire periodic table of elements in alphabetical order, Uncle Newt was not good at remembering the names of Nick and Tesla's friends.)

Nick pointed at a link that led to a webpage about Louis XIV. "I think he's the connection."

"Dude," Silas said, "did you miss the 'dead' part of 'dead king'? France must be up to their fiftieth Louis by now."

"I'm not saying Louis XIV is who we're looking for," Nick said. "I'm saying whoever owns the house next door must have used the guy's name for a reason. Just like the handbag company did, or the people who own the racehorse."

"What's so special about Louis XIV?" DeMarco asked.

"Let's find out," said Uncle Newt. He clicked on the link to the Louis XIV page. When it came up, he started reading it aloud.

He didn't get very far.

"Louis XIV of France, sometimes called Louis the Great or the Sun King—"

"That's it!" Nick and Tesla said together.

"What's it?" asked Silas.

"Sun King," Tesla told him. "You know—because we think the bad guys want to somehow use space-based solar power."

"And probably not to cook hot dogs," Nick added.

Silas nodded. "Oh, I get it. It's almost like a supervillain name. 'Behold, the sizzling, searing might and majesty of . . . *Sun King*!'" He thrust a fist at DeMarco and started making laser noises. "Pshew! Pshew!"

"Aggggggh! Nooooooo!" DeMarco cried, pretending to melt.

Nick and Tesla ignored them.

"Does it say *why* he was called the Sun King?" Nick said.

Uncle Newt scrolled down the page, passing a portrait of the famous French king. He was a pudgy man with a mass of curly black hair reminiscent of a heavy metal guitarist. He was dressed in what looked like white pantyhose on his stocky legs, and thrown over his shoulders was a flowing blue-and-white robe so ridiculously oversized it could have carpeted half the house.

"Here we go," Uncle Newt said. "'Louis XIV chose the sun as the symbol for his rule because it was associated with Apollo, god of the arts, knowledge, and light. He also believed in absolute monarchy—meaning that he could do anything he pleased—and pictured himself as the life-giving sun around which France revolved.'"

DeMarco (who was done melting) snorted. "How humble."

Silas (who was done *pshew*ing) shrugged. "No one's gonna tell the king he sounds like a jerk."

Nick and Tesla kept on ignoring them.

"The *why* doesn't seem to tie in with Mom and Dad," said Nick.

"I agree," said Tesla. "But we've still got the name to go on. Uncle Newt, can you search for just 'Sun

King'?"

Uncle Newt said something that sounded like "Absolumoe." "That's French for 'I'm on it!'" he said as he typed. "More or less."

A new page of results appeared on-screen. Among other things, it seemed, "Sun King" was a song by the Beatles, a brewery in Indianapolis, and a Chinese restaurant.

"Now we're getting somewhere!" Silas declared. "That Chinese place is in Stockton. That's less than an hour from here. Let's go!"

"You're just saying that because you're hungry," said DeMarco.

"No, I'm not," Silas said, pouting. He put his hands on his belly. "Although I did think I was going to eat a hot dog by now."

"Try 'Sun King Solar Power,'" Tesla said to her uncle. (When it came to Silas and DeMarco, she was still in ignore mode.)

"Wow. That's a popular name," Nick said when a fresh set of results popped up on-screen. "It looks like half a dozen companies are calling themselves 'Sun King.'"

"But only one's a neighbor," Uncle Newt said.

He pointed at a line among the search results: it was a link to a list of tenants at an industrial office park. "Sun King Solar Solutions in Mountain View, California. That's right down the road in Silicon Valley, where all the big tech companies have their headquarters."

"Can you look up their website?" Nick asked.

"Absolumoe," Uncle Newt said again, his fingers already flying across the keys. This time when the results came up, he blinked in surprise.

"Huh. That's weird," he said.

"What is?" said DeMarco. He and Silas peered at the screen. All they saw was just another list of links.

"I don't see anything," said Silas.

"That's just it," said Uncle Newt. "There's nothing to see. All the links are for other companies with similar names. Sun King Solar Solutions doesn't even have a website."

Nick and Tesla looked at each other. "A solar-power company in Silicon Valley that doesn't have a website?" Nick said skeptically.

"It's bogus," Tesla said firmly. "They're definitely who we're looking for. They must be."

Uncle Newt's hairless cat Eureka jumped onto

the dining room table, sauntered over to the laptop, and sat on the keyboard, sending Google on a search for "dfe234sqwadr."

"Well," Uncle Newt said, moving his hands away from the cat's firmly planted butt, "I don't know if it's really so sinister that Sun King Solar Solutions doesn't have a website, but I suppose I should check it out."

"*You* should check it out?" Tesla said.

"*Oui.* Drive down to Mountain View and take a look at their office."

"The 'check it out' part I understood," said Tesla. "It was the 'you' part I was wondering about."

"You think I ought to call the police?" Uncle Newt asked. "What am I going to say? 'My niece and nephew have a vague suspicion based on five minutes of surfing the Web. Could you send a patrol car to this address?'"

Nick placed a hand on his uncle's shoulder.

"I don't think Tesla was suggesting you send someone else," he said. "I think she meant 'Why can't *we* check the place out?' Plural."

"Ohhhh. You mean I should bring you guys along?"

"Yeah!" the kids cheered.

"No way," Uncle Newt said quickly.

The cheering stopped abruptly.

"Why not?" DeMarco asked.

"Because, I may be irresponsible, reckless, and imprudent," Uncle Newt said. "But I'm not *that* irresponsible, reckless, and imprudent."

"Yes, you are!" said Silas. Nick and Tesla shot him a glare that said, "You're not helping."

"Think about the summer we've had, Uncle Newt," Tesla said. "In the past month, we've rescued a little girl from kidnappers,[5] defeated an army of robot robbers,[6] captured a ring of spies,[7] and thwarted the sabotage of both a major museum[8] and a big Hollywood movie.[9] I think we can handle a visit to an office park."[10]

"Well . . ." said Uncle Newt.

"And we'd stay out of the way till you were sure the place was safe," Nick jumped in. "We could even come up with some kind of signal so you can tell us if the coast is clear. Of course, we'd have to assume that cell phones and Wi-Fi might be blocked or monitored, so it would have to be something that didn't rely on any kind of broadcast signal."

Uncle Newt looked intrigued—just as Nick had hoped. "Hmmm," he said. "That's an interesting challenge. If we can't use radio waves, maybe we could use electromagnetic radiation within the

---

5   *Nick and Tesla's High-Voltage Danger Lab.*—The authors

6   *Nick and Tesla's Robot Army Rampage.*—The authors

7   *Nick and Tesla's Secret Agent Gadget Battle.*—The authors

8   *Nick and Tesla's Super-Cyborg Gadget Glove.*—The authors

9   *Nick and Tesla's Special Effects Spectacular.*—The authors

10   Are you tired of footnotes yet? Because we are.—The authors

visible spectrum instead."

"Radiation?" DeMarco said, alarmed.

"I don't want to be a mutant!" said Silas.

Nick sighed. "Electromagnetic radiation within the visible spectrum is *light*," Tesla explained.

"Oh," said DeMarco.

"Why couldn't he just say that?" said Silas.

Tesla shrugged. "Cuz it sounds more sciencey the other way . . . ?"

"We've got tons of LEDs around the house," Nick told his uncle. "Could we use those somehow?"

"It's getting pretty late," Tesla added. "LEDs wouldn't be much good as signals when the sun's out, but once it's dark . . ."

Uncle Newt nodded thoughtfully. "Perhaps . . . yes . . . I like it . . ."

"Maybe we could figure out some way to give them lift, too," Nick suggested. "So they'd be visible from a distance."

Uncle Newt kept nodding. "Lift . . . yes . . . I *love* it."

He pushed back his chair and hopped to his feet so suddenly that Eureka yowled with fright and scrambled off the table.

"Where's he going?" Silas asked as Uncle Newt

strode purposefully out of the room.

"Where do you think?" Tesla said.

She and Nick looked at each other and grinned. Then they hurried after their uncle, following him up the hall, through the kitchen, and down the stairs to the laboratory.

PING-PONG BALL SIGNAL CANNON

THE STUFF

- Two sections of PVC pipe labeled 2½ inches, one 7 inches (18 cm) long and one 5 inches (13 cm) long (Note: Check that a ping-pong ball can fit in the pipe before you proceed!)

- A PVC T-connector that fits the pipes

- 8 balloons (the long, narrow, stretchy kind used to make balloon animals)

- A few feet of nylon "p-cord" rope (available at hardware stores and hobby shops) or a long, thick shoelace

- Ping-pong balls

- Duct tape

- LED bulbs of various colors, the brightest you can find

- Several #2032 3-volt button batteries (you'll need one to go with each LED you use)

- Plastic wrap

- Scissors

- A hobby knife or box cutter

- A nail or toothpick

- Safety goggles

- A responsible adult

THE SETUP

1. Assemble the PVC pieces as shown to form the signal cannon. If needed, fasten the connections using glue designed for plastic.

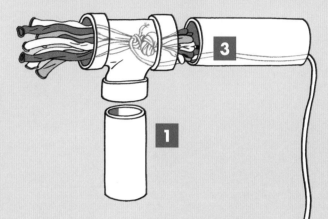

2. Line up the ends of the balloons. Tie them in a knot near the closed ends, leaving at least 4 inches (10 cm) of balloon free. Tie one end of the p-cord around the balloons, just next to the knot, on the long side, as shown.

3. As shown in the first Illustration, slip the free end of the cord, and the balloon knot, into the T-connector. The free ends of the balloons should hang out the front of the cannon. Spread the ends evenly around the opening of the pipe and tape

them in place, leaving about 2 inches (5 cm) of balloon length inside the pipe. Trim the free ends of the balloons.

4. Tie a loop in the free end of the p-cord to form a handle.

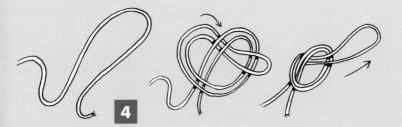

THE FINAL STEPS

1. For each signal, tape an LED bulb to a battery, with one wire touching each side of the battery. The longer wire should touch the positive (+) side of the battery; if the bulb doesn't light, switch the sides that the wires touch.

2. Ask your responsible adult to use the knife or box cutter to cut a slit in a ping-pong ball slightly larger than the battery. Carefully place the lit LED and battery into the ping-pong ball, squeezing the ball just enough to widen the slit and fit them inside. Once they're in, stuff the ball with enough plastic wrap to keep the battery from rattling around. You can use a nail or toothpick to pack the wrap in place.

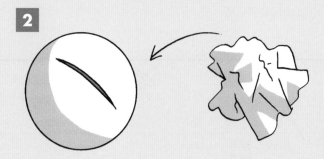

3. Your signal cannon is ready to fire! Put on your safety goggles and go outside. Point the launcher upward and place

the ping-pong ball loosely into the front of the launcher. (Don't push the ball down; let it rest on top of the balloons.)

4. DON'T POINT THE CANNON AT ANYONE! BE SAFE!!!

5. To launch a flare, pull back hard on the cord handle and quickly release it. The knot inside will hit the ping-pong ball and send it flying into the air. Practice to find the best way to launch for maximum distance and height. During the day, you can use regular, unlit ping-pong balls. They usually fly even higher.

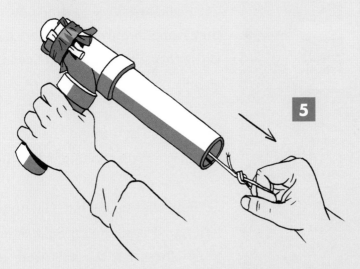

6. A tip to shoot your signals even farther: Ask a helper to place the ping-pong ball on the launcher while you pull the cord. But don't forget Final Step number 4: Be careful and stay safe!

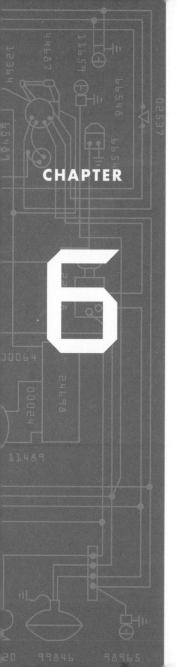

Though plenty of LEDs were indeed stashed around the house, they came in only three colors. So Uncle Newt proposed the following signals.

If he shot up a blue LED, it meant that he'd found the offices of Sun King Solar Solutions and the coast was clear.

If he shot up a white LED, then he'd found the Sun King Solar Solutions offices but the kids were to keep their distance.

And if he shot up a red LED, they were to run for their lives (and send help for him if they made it).

Nick and Tesla nodded, satisfied but a little un-nerved when Uncle Newt explained the meaning of the red signal. The three of them were still in the basement laboratory, going over the signals with Uncle Newt while Silas and DeMarco waited up-stairs. (The pair was freaked out by the lab's buzz-ing, sizzling machines and ooze-covered test tubes. And by the HAZARDOUS, POISON, and HIGH VOLTAGE signs on the door.)

"That'll work," Tesla said. "Let's pack up the launcher and—"

"But I wasn't done," Uncle Newt said.

And so he went on:

If he shot up a blue LED followed by a red one, it meant that he'd found Nick and Tesla's parents and all was well.

If he shot up a blue LED and then a white one, it meant that he'd found Nick and Tesla's parents but the kids should keep lying low.

If he shot up two blue LEDs in quick succession, it meant that he'd found Nick and Tesla's parents but the kids should contact the authorities immediately.

But if he shot up a blue LED followed by a white one, a red one, and then another blue one, it meant that the kids should—

That's when Nick cut him off. "These are getting pretty complicated," he said. "Couldn't we just stick with the first three?"

Uncle Newt held up a sheet of notebook paper he'd been scribbling on. On it was a very, very long list.

"But I've got so many more!" Uncle Newt protested. "You'd be amazed how much you can say with combinations of just three colors."

"You're not supposed to amaze us. You're supposed to tell us whether the place is safe or not," Tesla pointed out. "Anything more than that is just going to be confusing."

Uncle Newt's shoulders sagged. "I guess you're right," he said. He folded the sheet of paper and stuffed it into the breast pocket of his stain-speckled lab coat. "We ought to go, then. The sun's probably down already."

They loaded the cannon and a dozen LED-stuffed ping-pong balls into the only backpack in the house—a pink one with a drawing of a wide-eyed kitten and the words AIN'T I JUST THE CUTEST? embroidered on the back. Uncle Newt slung the backpack over one shoulder and led Nick and Tesla up the stairs and out the back door.

Uncle Newt was right about the sun having set. It was dusk.

Silas and DeMarco fell in behind and the group walked around the house, eventually reaching the large, ungainly vehicle parked in the driveway.

Uncle Newt had built the Newtmobile himself, which was why it looked like a cross between a jeep, a fishing boat, and a big green brick. He climbed in behind the wheel; Silas quickly called shotgun. The rest of the kids squeezed into the back seat.

Uncle Newt brought the vehicle roaring to life, backed out, and drove all of two blocks before pulling over and shutting off the engine.

"Why are we stopping?" DeMarco asked.

Uncle Newt nodded at two nearby houses.

"That's where you and Cyrus live, isn't it?" he said.

"Yeah?" said Silas. "So?"

DeMarco figured it out more quickly. "Oh, come on!" he said. "You can't leave us behind!"

"Sorry. I'm not going to put a couple eleven-year-olds in danger," Uncle Newt said.

"What about them?" DeMarco said, jerking a thumb at Nick and Tesla.

Uncle Newt shrugged. "That's different. They're family."

"Fair enough," Silas said (though if asked what was so fair about endangering one's relatives, he wouldn't've been able to tell you). "But consider this: DeMarco and I aren't eleven. We're twelve!"

"Oh, really? Twelve?" Uncle Newt said. He mulled over this new information but still shook his head. "Nah. Maybe if you were thirteen. Sorry. Out."

Silas opened the passenger door and slid from his seat.

"Awww, man," he said, moaning. "This is so bogus."

"Let us know how it goes," DeMarco said to Nick and Tesla. And then he got out, too.

"Don't get killed without us!" Silas called as the Newtmobile pulled away.

"That sounds like you want them to wait to get killed until we're there to get killed with them," DeMarco said.

"Oh. Right." Silas cupped his hands around his mouth and bellowed with all of his considerable might. "I MEAN, DON'T GET KILLED AT ALL!!!"

Several porch lights came on along the block, and a dog howled mournfully in the distance.

"Why can't you just say 'Good luck' like a normal person?" Silas said with a sigh.

"All right. I will." Silas sucked in a deep breath and cupped his hands around his mouth again.

"Don't bother," DeMarco said, nodding at the now empty street. "They're already gone."

Nick and Tesla couldn't do much planning on the way to the Sun King Solar Solutions headquarters in Mountain View. The Newtmobile had a fold-up convertible top that Uncle Newt had motorized because, as he put it, "Why the heck not?"

The answer to his supposedly rhetorical question being, "Because if it breaks we won't be able to get the top up at all." Which is why, as they sped down the highway, with their hair flying wildly in the wind, conversation was limited to "I CAN'T HEAR MYSELF THINK!" and "WHAT DID YOU SAY?" and "I ATE A BUG!" and "I HATE CONVERTIBLES!"

After about half an hour on the road, they pulled off the interstate and into a town that was larger, busier, and more immaculately manicured than funky little Half Moon Bay. As the name promised, there were mountains to view in the town of Mountain View (though at this time of the evening they were just black blobs that blotted out the horizon). Nearby were well-groomed lawns and tall palm and eucalyptus trees and ultramodern office buildings adorned with familiar names spelled out in big, glowing letters.

Netscape. Google. Symantec. Mozilla. Froofroo. Cheezel. Splonk!

(Nick and Tesla hadn't heard of Froofroo, Cheezel, or Splonk!, but the companies had impressive-looking logos on the signs in front of their even more impressive-looking offices.)

They saw no sign for Sun King Solar Solutions, however, even when they pulled up to the address Uncle Newt had found online: 1527 Harrington Avenue.

The property was no sleek, stylish, smoked-glass-and-chrome office complex. It was a rusty, dumpy warehouse surrounded by other rusty, dumpy warehouses and a large, dark parking lot.

"Doesn't look very high-tech," Tesla said.

"Looks can be deceiving," said Uncle Newt. "About ten minutes from here is the garage where Steve Jobs and Steve Wozniak built the first Apple computer. That place doesn't look very impressive, either."

"Maybe," Nick said, nodding at the shabby, shadowy warehouses. "But I bet it doesn't look like someplace Dr. Frankenstein would hang out."

Uncle Newt circled around and parked on the street; he and Nick and Tesla sat in silence and watched the parking lot for a while. No one came or went. Every so often a car would zip past on Harrington Avenue, but other than that, they seemed to be completely alone.

Eventually, Uncle Newt reached into the back of the Newtmobile and picked up the kitty-cat backpack.

"Well, I guess it's time to get this show on the road," he said. "Remember—don't come any closer unless you see the red LED signal."

"I thought we were supposed to run away if we saw the red signal," Nick said.

Uncle Newt shook his head. "No. That's the white signal."

Tesla shook *her* head. "No. White means we're supposed to stay where we are."

Uncle Newt rubbed his chin. "Really? I thought that was blue."

"Blue means the coast is clear," said Nick.

"I don't think so," said Uncle Newt.

"Look," Tesla said, "let's keep it simple. Blue is good. Red is bad. OK?"

"What about white?" Uncle Newt asked.

Tesla shrugged. "We don't need it."

Uncle Newt looked crestfallen. "But we made the white LED ping-pong balls! It would be a shame not to use them. Why don't we say that white means—"

"Uncle Newt!" Nick cried. "The longer we sit here talking, the more likely someone's going to spot us!"

"Good point."

Uncle Newt got out of the Newtmobile and slammed the door so hard, it made Nick wince.

"Try to be a little sneaky, Uncle Newt," Tesla said helpfully. "You know: Quiet. Inconspicuous."

"Hey—when am I ever conspicuous?" Uncle Newt said.

He flashed his niece and nephew a reassuring smile. But the twins would've been more reassured if the smile wasn't coming from a man with a raging case of bedhead wearing a filthy, scorch-marked lab coat and a T-shirt with YOU'RE WITH GENIUS ↑ printed across the front in neon-yellow letters.

"All right," Uncle Newt said, slapping his hands together. (At the loud clap, Nick winced again.) "Time to find your parents."

Uncle Newt gave Nick and Tesla a thumbs-up and then turned and headed toward the warehouses. Once in the parking lot, he hunched over and started crouch-walking in a serpentine pattern across the cracked asphalt.

"Uhh . . . is that supposed to be stealthy?" Nick asked.

"I guess," said Tesla.

They were both tempted to shout "Stand up straight and *hurry!*" but that would have just drawn more attention.

Eventually, Uncle Newt swerved around the corner of the nearest warehouse and ducked out of sight.

"Of course," said Tesla, "if the bad guys *are* in

there, then Uncle Newt might not even have time to send us a signal before they grab him."

"We promised to wait here," Nick said.

"We've done a lot more sneaking around this summer than Uncle Newt has," Tesla said. "We've gotten pretty good at it. If we followed him, just to keep an eye on him, he'd probably never know."

"We promised to wait here," Nick said again.

"We didn't solve all those mysteries this summer by sitting around waiting for someone else to do the work," Tesla retorted, trying to convince her brother. "And this time, it's personal."

"We promised to—"

A small, white ball of light shot out from somewhere behind the warehouses, arcing across the parking lot.

"Let's go!" Tesla said.

She jumped out of the Newtmobile and charged across the street.

Nick hesitated only a moment before dashing after his sister.

"What does the white LED even mean?" he asked as he followed her toward the warehouses.

"I have no idea!"

Up ahead, a red ball of light rocketed into the sky.

"I know what that means, though!" Tesla said.

"Me, too!" said Nick. "Trouble!"

Yet neither one slowed down. They reached the corner where their uncle had disappeared just as a third light—this time, a blue one—soared overhead.

"*What is going on?*" said Nick.

As they rounded the corner, Nick and Tesla found their uncle Newt calmly returning the LED cannon to his kitty backpack.

"Hey, kids," he said with a nonchalant wave when he noticed the twins gasping for air a few feet away. "I couldn't remember which color meant what, so I just used them all."

Nick rolled his eyes and sighed.

Tesla gritted her teeth and growled.

"Did you find something?" Nick asked.

"Yes and no. Come on. I'll show you."

Uncle Newt turned and headed toward the warehouse marked 1527. He led Nick and Tesla around the nearest corner and then stopped at a door. It had a window, and white words were stenciled on the glass.

SUN KING SOLAR SOLUTIONS

Tesla pushed on the door—*Why not try?* she figured—but it was locked. She cupped her hands to the glass and peered inside. Nick stepped up beside her and did the same.

The only light in the room was coming from a street lamp throwing a dull glow from behind them. But one thing was obvious despite the gloom and shadows inside.

The place was deserted. There were no desks, no chairs, no filing cabinets. Nothing on the walls. Nothing on the floor—not even carpet.

"Great," Nick said with a groan. "They went out of business."

"If they were ever really in business to begin with," said Tesla. "This could have just been a . . . a . . . What do you call it when someone starts a fake company?"

"A prank?" Uncle Newt suggested.

Tesla shook her head.

Uncle Newt tried again. "A joke? A gag? A trick? A caper? A lark?"

Tesla kept shaking her head.

"A front," Nick said.

Tesla nodded. "A front company. That's it. When someone wants to, you know, do businessy stuff without anyone knowing who it is."

Uncle Newt looked at his niece and nephew in amazement. "How do you two know so much about white-collar crime?"

"You'd be surprised what you can pick up from Nancy Drew and the Hardy Boys," Nick said.

"Unfortunately, there's no way to tell if we're right," said Tesla. "For all we know, this was a real company that closed down months ago."

Nick—aka "Little Mr. Sunshine," aka "Mr. Worst-Case Scenario"—couldn't resist summing up what that meant. "And that means we've been wasting our time . . . and we're out of clues."

"I didn't say that," Tesla shot back. She stepped to the side and bent down, hoping a different angle might reveal something new inside the abandoned office. "We'd just have to—hey!"

Something had crunched underfoot when she moved.

Tesla looked down and saw a small piece of

yellow paper sticking out from under her shoe. She moved her foot and picked it up. As she smoothed out the paper, she saw that it was perfectly square, with a sticky strip running along one side.

A Post-it note. And written on it were four words:

THEY KNEW YOU WERE

Nick gasped. "That's Mom's handwriting!"

"Are you sure?" Uncle Newt asked.

"Of course I'm sure! I've seen a million things written in that writing! Grocery lists. 'Happy birthday!' 'Please excuse Nick from gym—he's not feeling well.' I'm telling you, our mom wrote that. I'm sure of it."

"Me, too," said Tesla. Her voice cracked in a way she wasn't expecting, and her hands began to tremble. The note she was holding was the closest she'd come to her parents in weeks. It was the only proof the twins had that at least one of them was still alive.

Nick put a hand on her shoulder. She looked at her brother and gave him a stiff "I'm all right" nod. The trembling stopped.

"They knew you were?" Uncle Newt said, reading over Tesla's shoulder. "Does that mean anything to you two?"

"Not by itself," Tesla said. "I think Mom started a message she didn't have time to finish."

She glanced over again at Nick. His widened eyes told her that she didn't have to tell him what she was thinking. He was thinking the same thing.

Their mother had been there. She'd been there *that day*. They'd missed her by hours . . . perhaps mere minutes. And as she'd been forced to leave, she'd tried to leave her children a message . . . and a warning.

THEY KNEW YOU WERE COMING

Uncle Newt seemed to figure out what the message on the Post-it really meant about two seconds after his niece and nephew.

"Uhh, kids . . . I think we should go," he said, glancing over his shoulder at the impenetrable black shadows at the far corners of the parking lot. "Now."

He didn't really need to add the "Now."

Nick and Tesla were already running.

"Do you think the house is bugged?" Tesla shouted at her brother.

They were on the interstate headed back to Half Moon Bay, and once again the cool night air whipping past the roofless Newtmobile created a deafening roar.

"What?!" Nick shouted back.

"DO YOU THINK THE HOUSE IS BUGGED?!"

Nick pointed to his ears and shrugged.

"I think she's asking if you drink from the mouse's jug!" Uncle Newt hollered from the driver's seat. "Whatever that means."

"*What?*" Nick said again.

"Do you drink from the mouse's jug?" Uncle Newt yelled.

"I don't understand!"

"NEVER MIND!" Tesla roared.

No one spoke for the next half mile. Then Nick elbowed his sister in the ribs.

"Hey," he said, "do you think the house is bugged?"

"*What?*" said Tesla.

The second that Uncle Newt pulled off the interstate onto the last stretch of winding road leading home, the roar of the wind died down to a mild whoosh. Nick and Tesla turned to each other.

"Do you think the house is bugged?" they said in unison.

"Jinx!" Uncle Newt said. He counted quickly from one to ten and then said, "One of you owes me a Coke."

"What are you talking about?" said Tesla.

Uncle Newt blinked at his niece and nephew in the rearview mirror. "Don't you know that game?"

"What game?" said Nick.

"Oh. Well," said Uncle Newt, "never mind."

He returned to concentrating on the darkened road ahead.

"Anyway," Tesla said to her brother, "how do you think they knew we were coming?"

"I don't know. There's all kinds of ways they could be keeping track of us. Spies. Homing devices. Satellites. Hacking into . . . of course!" Nick slapped his own forehead. "I'm an idiot!"

"Only occasionally," said Tesla. "There's no need to beat yourself up for it."

"Tez—think about it! Where did we do the research that led us to that office? How did we find out where it was?"

"On the—oh . . . I get it!"

Tesla gave her brother a glare that communicated that he had her permission to slap himself in the head again.

"Are you saying the laptop's been hacked?" Uncle Newt asked.

"I opened a weird e-mail yesterday," Nick said sheepishly. "At first, it seemed like it was about Mom and Dad. Then we thought it was spam. But now—"

"It was spyware," Tesla said. "Which usually means some company or crook is trying to invade your privacy and steal your data. But in our case, it was sent by real spies!"

Nick sank low in his seat. "Sorry," he mumbled.

"No need to apologize, Nick." Uncle Newt said. "It was an accident. Could've happened to anybody. And in the end, all you did was infect my computer with malware that allowed the bad guys to track our every move and foil our only real shot at rescuing your parents. It's not the end of the world."

Nick whimpered.

"You can stop telling him not to feel bad," Tesla told her uncle. "He feels bad enough already."

Uncle Newt looked at Nick in his rearview mirror and saw that his reassurances hadn't been very reassuring.

"Nick," he said softly, "you made a mistake. It's OK. Scientists make mistakes all the time. Experiments fail, hypotheses are proved incorrect. And each and every time that happens, it's another step toward success because it's another opportunity to learn. So the laptop was hacked—that's information. If we think hard enough, we can figure out how to use it to our advantage."

Nick sat silently for a moment, absorbing his uncle's reasoning. Then he smiled. "Thanks," he said. "That helps me feel better."

Uncle Newt smiled back. "I guess I must be getting better at this wise, responsible adult thing, huh?" he said. "Now who wants ice cream and Pop-Tarts before we go to bed?"

The next morning, a bleary-eyed Nick and Tesla stumbled downstairs to find Uncle Newt at the dining room table eating ice cream and Hot Pockets for breakfast. (They'd eaten all the Pop Tarts the night before.)

"You know, I've been thinking," Uncle Newt said, dipping his pepperoni pizza pocket into a bowl of rocky road. "If the laptop is sending out information about us, it can be traced to an IP address—the location of the computer that's hacking in. Our enemies might think they're spying on us, but they could be leading us right to them."

Nick's droopy eyes were suddenly wide open. "Really? You can do that?"

"Who, me?" said Uncle Newt. "No. I'm no hacker."

Nick slumped. "Oh."

"Then who?" Tesla said.

"I was thinking of Agent McIntyre and Agent Doyle," said Uncle Newt. "I don't know if they work for the CIA, the FBI, or the YMCA. But whoever it is must have programmers who can crack that spyware and see where it leads."

"Makes sense," said Tesla, sounding a bit surprised, given the source.

"But if we go to Agent McIntyre and Agent Doyle, we'll have to admit we ignored their warning," Nick said. "They're gonna be mad."

Tesla scowled and shook her head dismissively. "So? It's their own fault for not telling us everything. If they didn't keep so many secrets, we wouldn't have to take matters into our own hands."

"I guess so," Nick muttered. "It's too bad we can't bug *them*."

Tesla spun so sharply that Nick yelped, recoiling in surprise.

"What did you say?"

"Uh, it's too bad we can't bug them?" Nick repeated uncertainly. "You know, so we could find out everything they haven't been telling us?"

"That's it!" Tesla cried. "Brilliant plan! I love it!"

"Umm . . . it was more a wish than a plan."

But Tesla was no longer listening. She turned from her brother and hunched over, fingers pressed to her temples as if she were trying to squeeze inspiration from her head by sheer force. "How do we do it?" she asked herself. "How, how, how?"

The doorbell rang, and since Tesla was still muttering "How, how, how?" and Uncle Newt was scooping up more ice cream with the last soggy corner of his Hot Pocket, it was Nick who went to answer.

"Look who's here," he said when he returned a moment later.

Following him into the dining room were Silas and DeMarco. The former was grinning; the latter was glowering.

"Ice cream for breakfast?" Silas said. "Lucky ducks!"

DeMarco whacked him on the arm. "What?" said Silas.

"We're mad, remember?" DeMarco said.

"Oh, yeah." Silas turned toward Nick and Tesla and Uncle Newt, his smile replaced by a scowl. "Thanks for keeping us in the loop," he said sarcastically.

"First you run off without us, and then you don't even bother letting us know you made it back alive," DeMarco added. "If you're going to keep us out of trouble, the least you can do is tell us about it afterward." DeMarco said "keep us out of trouble" as if it were a bad thing.

"Sorry, guys," said Nick. "We didn't get back till late."

"Just tell us what happened."

And so they did. Nick did most of the talking, with Tesla chiming in when she disagreed with her brother's description of the events. Uncle Newt got everyone ice cream.

"Whoa!" Silas said when Nick was done telling the story (and Tesla was done interrupting). "So if it hadn't been for that computer virus warning the bad guys, you might have rescued your parents!"

Nick winced. "The virus could still lead us to our mom and dad," he said. "We'll give the laptop to the agents, and hopefully they'll find a way to trace whatever messages or signals the virus has been sending."

"And while they're here, we're going to eavesdrop on them to find out what they haven't been telling us," Tesla said. She clapped her brother on the back. "That was Nick's plan."

Silas and DeMarco turned toward Nick.

"How are you going to get Agent McIntyre and Agent Doyle to come back here?" Silas asked him.

"I don't know," said Nick.

"How are you going to get them to talk when they think you're not around?" DeMarco asked.

"I don't know," said Nick.

"How are you going to eavesdrop on them?" Silas asked.

"I don't know," said Nick.

"Hmm," said DeMarco. "Sounds like more of a wish than a plan."

"That's what I said," Nick grumbled.

Silas took a step forward and put a hand up, his index finger pointing at the ceiling.

"I have a plan!" he declared. "Pen and paper! I must have pen and paper!"

"Look in the freezer. I saw a notepad in there when I was getting the ice cream," Uncle Newt said. "There are pens on the counter." Nobody bothered asking him why a notepad would be in the fridge. It was just that kind of house.

Silas marched into the kitchen and returned a few seconds later with a (very cold) legal pad in one hand and a marker in the other. He sat down at the dining room table and began to draw.

"This isn't going to be one of those crazy diagrams with you and an eagle doing something impossible, is it?"[11] Tesla asked.

"No," said Silas, pouting. "This isn't going to be like that at all."

A few minutes later, he proudly displayed his drawing to his friends:

11 See every other Nick and Tesla book.—The authors

Everyone gathered round and stared at the diagram.

"It's a little, ah, busy," said DeMarco.

"I'm not even sure where I'm supposed to look first," said Nick.

"I think I get it," Uncle Newt said. "Silas finds a dead squirrel in a tree, then uses it to lure his father to . . . no. Sorry. I'm lost."

"It's perfect," said Tesla.

Everyone gaped at her in shock—even Silas. "It is?" he said.

Tesla nodded. "Absolutely. I mean, I think it could be streamlined a bit. We don't really need the squirrel or the condor—"

"Awww," Silas said.

"—but other than that I think it's pretty solid," Tesla continued.

"Pretty solid?" said Nick. He pointed at the notepad in Silas's hands. "That?"

Again, Tesla nodded. "We put our pendants in one of the solar cookers, which brings Agents McIntyre and Doyle to see if you and I are really getting broiled. When they get to the house, we give them the laptop and tell them what we found in Mountain View. At the same time, someone's hiding a walkie-talkie near their SUV while Silas's dad blocks the car in. If we trap it between the Newtmobile, the house, and the trees lining the driveway, Agent McIntyre and Agent Doyle will be stuck. When they come out and realize they can't leave, we'll eavesdrop on everything they say. Maybe we could even whip up a solar-powered walkie-talkie so we don't have to worry about the batteries running out before we learn what we want to know."

Nick and DeMarco looked dubious. Uncle Newt looked confused.

"I still think it's better if we put the walkie-talkie on a condor," Silas said. "But your way might work."

"Wait, wait, wait," Nick said. "I have a question."

DeMarco glanced down at Silas's diagram. "Just one?" he said.

"For now," Nick said. "Silas, would your dad really help us block in Agent McIntyre's SUV?"

Silas nodded firmly. "Absolutely. You saved his comic book shop.[12] He owes you one. And it'll be to-

---

12 *Nick and Tesla's Robot Army Rampage.* We're hoping this is the last footnote, but you'll have to keep reading to find out.
—The authors

tally believable that his Rabbit broke down. It breaks down for real all the time."

"OK, if you say so," said Nick, sounding unconvinced. He turned to his uncle. "What do you think?"

Uncle Newt shrugged. "It's worth a try. But the only walkie-talkies I have lying around don't have a lot of range, and a solar-powered one would be bulky. We'll need to find a way to hide it if we're going to get it close enough to pick up a conversation."

"I've got it!" Silas burst out. "We'll disguise it as a condor nest!"

"Well . . ." said Uncle Newt.

"Hmm . . ." said DeMarco.

"Umm . . ." said Nick.

No one looked enthused about the plan. But Tesla smiled.

"Silas," she said, putting a hand on his shoulder, "I can't believe I ever doubted you."

Silas beamed.

SOLAR SPY BIRDHOUSE

THE STUFF

- A birdhouse (available at craft and hobby shops)*

- Hot-glue sticks

- Electrical tape

- A rubber band

- Double-sided tape

- Thin plastic-coated wire, like speaker wire or black and red electronic-project wire from a hobby shop

- 2 walkie-talkies that run on either 2 or 3 AA or AAA batteries**

- A solar panel***

*You can skip the birdhouse if you want, but you'll need some way to hang or place your gadget in the sun.

**A walkie-talkie that runs on a 9-volt battery won't work for this project. The less expensive the walkie-talkie, the better; pricier models have an auto-shutoff feature or will let you press the Talk button for only a certain amount of time.

***The cells of the solar panel need to have a voltage equal to that of the batteries your walkie-talkies use. Two batteries equal 3 volts. Three batteries equal 4.5 volts. Also, the solar panel should put out 1.5 watts of power or more. Small solar panels are available from hobby shops that sell parts for electronic projects; they are also available from online specialty stores and some large online retailers.

THE SETUP

1. Cut two hot-glue sticks the same length as the batteries used in the walkie-talkies. Cut two pieces of wire about 6 inches (15 cm) long. Strip about ½ inch (1.25 cm) of the plastic from each end.

2. Open the battery compartment of one walkie-talkie and find the metal tab marked with a plus sign (+). Place a wire against the tab and put one of the glue-stick pieces into the battery holder to keep the wire in place. Find the metal tab marked with a minus sign (–) in the battery container that's farthest from the wire you just attached. Place the other wire against this tab and hold it in place with the other glue stick.

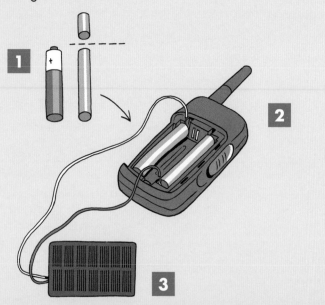

3. Connect the wire that you attached to the positive (+) tab of the walkie-talkie to the positive wire on the solar panel (usually red). Connect the negative (–) wire from the walkie-talkie to the negative wire on the solar panel (usually black).

4. Wrap the connections in electrical tape and replace the battery cover. Tape the glue sticks in place if it seems like they might fall out.

THE FINAL STEPS

1. Time to test the walkie-talkie. Go outside on a sunny day and hold the solar panel so that it faces the sun. You should be able to turn on the walkie-talkie; test it with the other (battery-powered) walkie-talkie to make sure they can transmit and receive audio. For the walkie-talkies to work, the solar panel must directly face the sun at all times.

2. Wrap the rubber band around the solar walkie-talkie tight enough to keep the Transmit button depressed. If necessary, place a piece of the hot-glue stick between the button and the rubber band. Use the double-sided tape to attach the solar walkie-talkie to the bottom of the birdhouse and the solar panel to the birdhouse roof.

3. Hang the birdhouse directly in the sunshine so that the sun's rays can power the walkie-talkie. As long as the walkie-talkie has enough sunlight, it should transmit audio.

4. Remember: Always use any listening device for good and not evil! And if a bird happens to make a nest in your spy birdhouse, enjoy the sounds of everyday bird life.

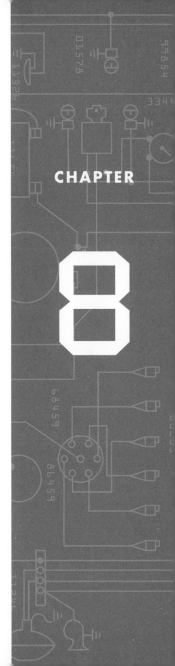

Uncle Newt had a cheap set of walkie-talkies he'd bought as a Christmas gift for his niece and nephew four years ago. He rummaged around the closets until he found the box and then handed it to Nick and Tesla. "And a happy new year!" he said. Then he headed to the basement.

"I was tinkering with a solar-powered lawn mower a while back," Uncle Newt explained as he clomped down the stairs. "But it kept—"

"Let me guess," interrupted Nick. "Exploding?"

NICK AND TESLA'S SOLAR-POWERED SHOWDOWN

"No, of course not!" Uncle Newt said. "It kept *melting.* Now, let's see . . ."

He opened a particularly musty, cobweb-covered cabinet in a darkened corner of the lab. He rooted around inside for a moment, tossed a microscope and a gas mask over his shoulder, and then turned around, holding a flat black rectangle.

"A photovoltaic cell solar panel," he announced. "Uses photons from sunlight to excite electrons, so they'll separate from their atoms and create a current that can be used as electricity. You know who made these puppies possible, don't you?"

"Uhh . . . Mr. Photovoltaic?" Tesla guessed. She knew she was wrong—*photo* referred to light, and *voltaic* to electricity—but she hadn't studied the history of solar power.

"Albert Einstein?" said Nick, who had.

"Exactly," said Uncle Newt, looking impressed. "Before he was famous, Einstein won a Nobel Prize for the work he did on light and how it can generate a flow of electrons from certain materials."

Nick nodded. "That was the breakthrough that made solar power possible, decades later."

"Showoff," Tesla muttered. "Anyway—we still

don't have a birdhouse."

"Sure we do," said Uncle Newt.

He returned to the cabinet, reached in again, threw out what looked like a Geiger counter and a sundial, and then turned holding a perfect blue birdhouse.

"Why do you have a birdhouse in your basement?" Nick asked as his uncle carried it to one of the worktables.

"It was for the mice. I wanted them to stop nesting in my beakers."

"Did it work?" asked Tesla.

Uncle Newt closed one eye and squinted into the birdhouse.

"Nope," he said. "Empty."

"Good. That means we won't have to evict any inhabitants," said Tesla. She picked up a screwdriver and said, "Let's build this thing."

DeMarco and Silas had gone home for a little while but returned and were waiting on the back porch until the solar spy birdhouse was ready.

"It's not big enough," Silas said when Nick, Tesla, and Uncle Newt finally joined them outside.

"What do you mean?" asked Uncle Newt, holding the birdhouse over his head. "Once this is up in a tree, the walkie-talkie and the solar panel will be totally hidden. See?"

Silas shook his head. "I mean, it's not big enough for a condor."

"It doesn't have to be big enough for a condor," Tesla said. "It's a plain old normal birdhouse. That's the point."

Silas scowled. "What's the fun of that?"

"It's not supposed to be fun," said Nick. "It's just supposed to work."

"I like fun," Silas grumbled.

Still holding the birdhouse up high, Uncle Newt walked off toward the row of oak trees that lined the driveway. DeMarco went with him, scouting for branches that were just the right height: close to the ground so the walkie-talkie could pick up conversations yet high enough to keep it out of sight.

"So," Tesla said to Silas, "is your dad up for this?"

Silas nodded reluctantly. "Yeah, but . . ."

"But what?" said Nick.

"When I told him you need to trap a couple government agents on your uncle's driveway for a while, he wanted me to swear that whatever we were up to wouldn't endanger national security. So I did."

"What's the problem?" asked Tesla.

"Well . . . that got me thinking. *Can* we be sure we aren't endangering national security?"

Nick and Tesla answered at the same time:

"Absolutely," said Tesla.

"Good question," said Nick.

Tesla glared at her brother.

He let her handle the rest of the conversation.

"Look," Tesla said, "we've done a better job tracking down these spies than Agent McIntyre and Agent Doyle, right? So if anyone's endangering national security, it's them—by refusing to tell us everything and let us help rescue our parents."

Slowly, a smile spread across Silas's broad face.

"Yeah," he said, nodding. "That makes sense."

"So, you're in?" said Tesla.

Silas continued to nod, adding a thumbs-up for good measure.

Nick gave his sister a thumbs-up, too.

"All right, then. You go help DeMarco and Uncle

Newt," Tesla said to Silas. Then she turned to Nick. "We should prep the solar cooker."

Nick pulled at the gold chain around his neck; with that, the star-shaped pendant/tracking device that Agent McIntyre had given him popped out from under his shirt.

"Guess it's time to heat things up," Nick said.

After the pendants had been in the cooker for twenty minutes, Nick said, "Maybe it's not hot enough for them to think we're in trouble."

"It's hot enough," said Tesla.

After the pendants had been in the cooker for thirty minutes, Nick said, "Maybe they're so mad about us tricking them last time that they've decided to let us fry."

"They haven't," said Tesla.

After the pendants had been in the cooker for forty minutes, Nick said, "Maybe—"

"Shhh," said Tesla. "Here they come."

And she was right.

The distant roar of an engine—a big one—

grew steadily louder. A moment later, a black SUV swerved, with tires squealing, into Uncle Newt's driveway. It screeched to a halt behind the Newtmobile. Right on target.

(As part of the plan, Silas and DeMarco were hiding in the bushes by the empty house next door, ready to move the birdhouse if the SUV stopped somewhere unexpected. Now they didn't have to bother. They could stay put until it was time to kick off Phase 2.)

The SUV's front doors swung open, and Agents McIntyre and Doyle jumped out and charged around the Newtmobile. They were dressed in their usual getups: black business suits and spotless white shirts. Both were reaching inside their jackets, presumably to whip out something lethal if the situation called for it.

The two agents stopped dead in their tracks when they saw Nick and Tesla waiting on the back porch, a hot dog cooker on the pavement between them.

"Told ya," Agent Doyle said to Agent McIntyre. "I'm just glad you didn't call the Coast Guard this time."

Agent McIntyre scowled first at Agent Doyle, then at Nick and Tesla, and then at the solar cooker.

"Your transponders are in that . . . thing?" she said.

"Transponders? You mean our pendants?" said Tesla. "Yeah, they're in there."

"We were just trying to get your attention," said Nick.

Agent McIntyre looked Nick in the eye so intently that he had to look away.

"Well, you got it," Agent McIntyre said. "And you destroyed your transponders in the process. They're not built to withstand those kinds of temperatures."

"Oh," Nick mumbled. "Oops."

"Look, we're sorry about the transponders and we're sorry we had to trick you into coming out here again," said Tesla, not sounding sorry in the slightest. "But we've got something important to show you. Follow me."

She started walking toward the back door.

Nick followed her.

Agent McIntyre and Agent Doyle stayed put.

Tesla spun around to face the agents.

"We can tell you exactly where our mother was

less than twenty-four hours ago," she said.

"And we can show you how to trace her to wher-ever she is now," Nick added.

Tesla pulled open the back door and gestured to-ward the kitchen, inviting Agent McIntyre and Agent Doyle inside.

"Coming?" she said.

The agents looked at each other. "We're already here," Agent Doyle said with a shrug. "And you've seen what they've managed to accomplish before."

"All right." Agent McIntyre turned toward Nick and Tesla. "But this better be good."

"Oh, it is," said Tesla. "Trust us."

As Agent McIntyre and Agent Doyle went inside, Silas and DeMarco popped out of the bushes by Ju-lie Casserly's old house. DeMarco took off running, headed for the street. Silas paused to give Nick and Tesla a grin and a thumbs-up.

Nick returned the thumbs-up.

Tesla shooed Silas away while mouthing one si-lent word.

"*Go.*"

Off he went.

Phase 2 was on.

Uncle Newt was waiting at the dining room table. Next to his chair was a blue plastic basket overflowing with wrinkled and stained T-shirts, lab coats, and jeans.

"You made us come all this way to show us your laundry?" asked Agent Doyle incredulously.

He and Agent McIntyre had stopped on the opposite side of the table, across from Uncle Newt.

"It's what's *in* the laundry that's important," Uncle Newt said as Nick and Tesla sat down on either side of him.

"If it's so important, why would it be in your laundry?" asked Agent McIntyre.

"Because it's been hacked," Uncle Newt said.

Agent Doyle narrowed his eyes. "Your laundry's been hacked?"

"No, no! The thing *in* my laundry. My laptop. We think whoever has captured Nick and Tesla's parents have been using it to spy on us. So I packed it in something that would muffle sound so it couldn't eavesdrop." Uncle Newt smiled sheepishly. "It's probably going to smell a bit when you take it out. Sorry."

"What makes you think someone's been using the laptop to spy on you?" Agent McIntyre asked.

"That," said Tesla. She pointed at the dining room table. The Post-it note with the message from her mother was sitting between a plate with a half-eaten Hot Pocket and an open box of Cap'n Crunch. (Uncle Newt was supposed to clear the table before Agents McIntyre and Doyle arrived, but apparently he'd forgotten.)

As the agents leaned forward to look at the note, Nick began telling them how and where they'd found it.

Their demeanors changed immediately. Agent Doyle was suddenly alert—engaged and intrigued.

Agent McIntyre was furious. "You have been meddling in a federal investigation!" she yelled, losing the last grip on her temper.

Nick and Uncle Newt shrank back in their seats.

Tesla nodded. "Yes, we have," she said coolly. "And very effectively, too."

"No. *Not* very effectively," Agent McIntyre snapped. "The spy ring we've been searching for was holding your mother, and probably your father, prisoner here in the Bay Area. Right under our noses. We would have found them eventually. But now they've moved your parents who knows where, thanks to your snooping!"

"Can't you trace them with that?" Nick asked meekly, poking a finger at the laundry basket. "The laptop, I mean. Not the dirty clothes."

Agent McIntyre glared at him with such obvious rage that Nick wanted to crawl out of his chair and hide behind it. But before she could bark out a reply, Agent Doyle spoke.

"We can try," he said. "*If* the laptop really has been hacked and *if* the people who hacked it have been sloppy about covering their tracks, then *maybe* we'll be able to find them."

"That's a lot of ifs," said Agent McIntyre. She'd had a moment to take a deep breath and get her anger under control, but still she sounded far from calm. "And I'll give you one more: *If* you can't stay out of the way, then we will *put* you out of the way."

"What's that supposed to mean?" asked Tesla.

"It means," said Agent Doyle, "that McIntyre might have made a mistake letting you two stay with your uncle while we sorted out this situation. One more wild-goose chase and we'll have to take you into protective custody. You don't want that to happen, believe me. You're a lot more comfortable here."

As Agent Doyle spoke, Agent McIntyre walked around the table, picked up the laundry basket, and headed for the back of the house.

"Can I get a receipt for that?" Uncle Newt asked.

"No," Agent McIntyre said without slowing down.

"Aw, man," Uncle Newt groaned. "Some of my favorite T-shirts are in there."

Agent Doyle picked up the Post-it note, stuffed it in his shirt pocket, and followed Agent McIntyre without another word.

Nick and Tesla looked at each other. The agents had stormed out of the house more quickly than they'd anticipated. Would Phase 2 be ready?

The twins hopped up and scurried out after them.

"Will you at least promise to let us know if you trace the spyware to the bad guys?" Tesla called out.

"No," said Agent McIntyre.

"The only thing we can promise," said Agent Doyle, "is that you'll be sorry if you get in our way one more—oh, give me a break!"

The two agents stopped in the driveway and stared at the tiny, dented, boxy blue car that was parked all of two inches from their SUV's rear bumper, its engine rumbling and coughing. At the wheel was a burly, bearded man in a faded flannel shirt—Dave Kuskie, Silas's dad. Silas and DeMarco were squeezed into the teeny back seat behind him.

Mr. Kuskie rolled down the window and leaned out.

"Just who we were coming to see!" he said to Nick and Tesla, grinning.

"Sir, would you mind—?" Agent Doyle began.

"Just a sec," Mr. Kuskie said. "So, Nick, Tesla—we're going to a matinee of *Major Patriot: Super Commando*. You want to tag along?"

"It totally sets up the Metalman reboot!" Silas shouted. "You gotta come see it with us!"

"*Sir*," Agent McIntyre repeated, her anger rising, "we need you to move your vehicle so we can—"

"Hold your horses. This won't take long," said Mr. Kuskie. "What do you say, kids? Popcorn's on me!"

"Sorry," said Nick. "I'm not in the mood."

"Me, neither," said Tesla. "Thanks, though."

"Oh, come on!" DeMarco yelled. "If you don't go now, someone'll tell you all the spoilers before you can see it!"

"And that someone will be me!" Silas added gleefully.

Agent McIntyre took an angry step toward Mr. Kuskie's ancient car.

"Move that hunk of junk *now*," she said with a snarl.

Silas's dad truly looked at her for the first time.

"Excuse me?" he said. "Miss, this is a vintage 1982 Volkswagen Rabbit in mint condition. It is *not* a hunk of—"

The car's engine revved, sputtered, whined . . . and then died.

"Not again!" Silas cried.

"Come on, come on!" said DeMarco. "You know I hate to miss the previews!"

Mr. Kuskie looked down at the ignition and *seemed* to fiddle with the key.

Nothing happened.

"Uh-oh," said Mr. Kuskie.

"Uh-oh?" repeated Silas.

"I think the carburetor's out again," his father said.

Silas slapped his hands to the side of his face and wailed.

"Noooooooooooooooooooooo!"

"Booooooooooooooooooooooo!" said DeMarco.

"Knock it off, guys," said Mr. Kuskie. "*Major Patriot* will still be at the theater in a couple days."

"Booooooooooooooooooooo!" DeMarco said again. This time Silas joined him.

Their performance was a little *too* good: Mr. Kuskie looked like he wanted to turn around and throttle them. Instead, he got out of the car and started walking toward the house.

"Can I use your uncle's telephone to call the garage?" he asked Nick and Tesla. "I left my cell phone at home."

"Sure," Nick said.

"You can use the phone in the kitchen," added Tesla.

The twins started escorting Mr. Kuskie around to the back door. Silas and DeMarco got out of the Rabbit and stomped after them, trying to look sullen.

"A couple of days?" Silas whined. "How am I supposed to avoid all the spoilers for a couple of days?"

"Stay off the Internet?" DeMarco suggested.

Silas scoffed. "Don't be ridiculous."

Agent McIntyre and Agent Doyle watched them leave in slack-jawed disbelief.

"Where do you think you're going?" Agent McIntyre called after Mr. Kuskie.

"To call my mechanic, like I said," he said without slowing or turning around. "Don't worry—he's fast. He'll be here within an hour." He glanced back at the clothes basket. "The Laundromat won't close before you get there."

And then he and the kids rounded the corner of the house and were gone.

"But . . . but . . ." Agent McIntyre was left spluttering.

She looked at the Rabbit, the Newtmobile, the house, the trees, and—hopelessly boxed in by them all—her big, black, trapped SUV.

"You know," said Agent Doyle, "I almost wish those Holt kids really were being barbecued when we got here."

Agent McIntyre sighed.

"It's not too late," she said. "Got a match?"

Nick, Tesla, Silas, and DeMarco stampeded through the kitchen to join Uncle Newt in the dining room. He was at the table bent over the walkie-talkie he'd just retrieved from its hiding place—a box of dirty beakers and test tubes lying in the corner.

"What are they saying? What are they saying?" Nick said, panting.

"So far, just that they wouldn't mind setting you and your sister on fire," Uncle Newt reported.

"*What?*" said Mr. Kuskie from the kitchen, where his job was to pretend to call a garage and, more important, cut off Agent McIntyre and Agent Doyle if they tried to come in the back door.

"I'm pretty sure they're joking," Uncle Newt said. "Probably . . . hopefully."

"They better be joking," said Mr. Kuskie. "I'm not thrilled about annoying a couple of government agents."

"Oh, don't be a wimp, Dad," said Silas. "You annoy people all the time."

"Not people who could get me audited!"

Silas and the other kids pressed in around the table, hovering over Uncle Newt. For a moment, no sound came from the walkie-talkie except a low, staticky hiss.

DeMarco cocked his head and leaned over the table.

"I think I hear them," he said. "It's muffled, though. Like they're talking with pillows over their faces."

Tesla crept to the nearest window, pulled back the curtain, and peeped out.

"Oh, great. They got in their SUV. That's why we can barely hear them."

Nick picked up the walkie-talkie and turned the

volume as high as it would go. The crackling static got louder—but so did a pair of faint, garbled voices.

Nick brought the walkie-talkie close to his ear.

"[Something something] that note [something something] be planted [something something] a trick," he heard Agent Doyle say.

"[Something something] don't think so [something something] the laptop [something something] move fast," said Agent McIntyre.

"[Something something] find any malware [something something] best lead [something something] days," Agent Doyle said. "[Something something] better call [something something] and LET THEM KNOW WHAT WE'RE BRINGING IN."

Nick yelped, dropped the walkie-talkie, and slapped his hands over his ears.

Agent Doyle's voice had gone from whisper-soft to foghorn-loud in the space of an instant.

"He's getting out of the SUV!" Tesla said. "Turn down the volume before he hears himself!"

Uncle Newt snatched the walkie-talkie off the floor and fiddled with a knob on the side.

For a moment, they heard no sound at all.

"Oh, no," said Nick, staring miserably at the walkie-talkie. "I broke it."

But then they made out an unmistakable sound: the slamming of a car door. It came in through both the window and the walkie-talkie.

Everyone sighed in relief.

"What's going on?" Mr. Kuskie called from the kitchen.

"It sounds like Doyle's about to call headquarters," DeMarco told him.

"Oh, man," Mr. Kuskie said. "I am in so much trouble."

"I don't think it has anything to do with you, Dad," Silas said. "He's just, like, reporting in."

But they could hear Mr. Kuskie mutter "Oh, man" again, and then he began pacing.

"He's taking out his cell phone and moving away from the driveway," Tesla reported from the window. "Now he's stopping. He's right under the branch with the birdhouse! We're going to hear every word!"

Uncle Newt and the kids traded triumphant smiles.

Their plan was working! And if it kept working, they were about to learn some of the secrets the agents had been keeping from them.

"Control, this is Doyle," they heard the agent say.

"You were right. The Scooby gang figured out that the laptop was hacked. But that's not the worst of it. Martha Holt left a note for them when you cleaned out the Mountain View office. They know she was there . . . and now McIntyre knows it, too. Those kids have forced our hand with their meddling. We have to give Option A another try before McIntyre finally sees the big picture."

Everyone's smiles faded.

"Oh, no," said Nick.

"Of course," said Tesla.

"No way," said DeMarco.

"Yes way, I'm afraid," said Uncle Newt.

"He calls us the Scooby gang?" said Silas.

The others stared at him.

"What?" Silas said.

"Don't you get it?" said Tesla. "Agent Doyle is a traitor. He's working for the bad guys!"

A moment of stunned silence passed as reality sank in for the group gathered in the dining room.

Agent Doyle was one of the bad guys.

Even the walkie-talkie was silent. Apparently, Doyle was listening to whomever he'd called—the person he'd referred to as "Control."

"Perfect," Agent Doyle said at last. "But hold off for now. I'm stuck at Newton Holt's house because . . . hang on. Someone's coming."

"Who is it?" DeMarco said to Tesla, who was still standing near the window.

She peeked around the curtain.

"No one's coming up the driveway," she said. "Maybe it's—no! Not yet!"

"What's going on?" asked Nick. "Who is it?"

Suddenly, another voice was heard over the walkie-talkie, providing the answer to Nick's question before Tesla could supply her own.

"You know what?" Mr. Kuskie was saying. "My mechanic told me that if I let the car sit for a few minutes, it should start right up. How about I give it try?"

"Dad?" Silas said. "What's he doing out there?"

"He lost his nerve," replied Tesla. "I don't think he even heard that Agent Doyle is a double agent."

A car door opened and slammed shut, and a moment later an engine sputtered to life.

"Well, what do you know? It worked!" Mr. Kuskie said. "I'll just back out, and you can be on your way. Sorry if I caused you any inconvenience. It would never be my intention to come between a fellow citizen and his or her important business."

"Oh, Dad," Silas groaned, hanging his head.

Another car door opened and closed, and a second engine started.

NICK AND TESLA'S SOLAR-POWERED SHOWDOWN

"They're leaving," Tesla said.

"We've got to warn Agent McIntyre!" Nick cried.

He bolted for the front door, with Tesla, Uncle Newt, Silas, and DeMarco fast on his heels. But they were too late. By the time they rushed outside, the black SUV was already off, cruising up the street. Mr. Kuskie was waving at it from his Rabbit, which he'd backed from the driveway and parked by the curb.

"Have a nice day!" he called out, waving to the disappearing vehicle. "God bless America!"

"With the pendants ruined, we have no way to contact Agent McIntyre again," Nick said. "We can't tell her about Agent Doyle."

"We've got to catch up to her, then," said Tesla. "Now."

Uncle Newt leapt from the front porch and ran to the driveway.

"To the Newtmobile!" he announced.

The kids scrambled after him.

As Uncle Newt slid behind the wheel of his homemade boat-car, Nick and Tesla climbed into the backseat. But when Silas and DeMarco attempted to follow their friends, Uncle Newt reached back and closed the door.

"Sorry, guys," he said. "I can only put my closest relatives in mortal danger, remember?"

"Please, please, please let us come, too!" begged Silas, clasping his hands together.

"You can't make us miss a real-life car chase!" DeMarco protested indignantly.

"Can and am," replied Uncle Newt. And with that he put the Newtmobile in reverse and barreled backward down the driveway.

Seconds later, he was whooshing up the street, heading in the same direction as Agents McIntyre and Doyle. But the SUV was nowhere in sight.

"I don't see them!" said Nick.

"They're probably headed for the interstate," said Uncle Newt. "Whether they're going north to San Francisco or south to San Jose, the highway would be quickest."

"But what if their HQ isn't in San Francisco or San Jose?" Nick asked. "If we go the wrong way, we'll lose them for good, and Agent McIntyre won't know that Agent Doyle is a turncoat until it's too late."

"Just go toward the interstate," Tesla said, cutting in. She turned to Nick and gave him a swat. "And stop with the worst-case scenarios. They don't help."

"Sorry," Nick said, rubbing his sore shoulder.

"Hold on!" Uncle Newt shouted (about a second too late to do his niece and nephew any good). "I've got to gun it if we're going to get through this light!"

They shot through an intersection—and out of Uncle Newt's neighborhood—just as the stop-light changed from yellow to red. The Newtmobile swerved left, tires squealing. Half a minute later, it was turning right onto the winding, climbing, two-lane road that led from Half Moon Bay to the interstate a few miles away.

Nick pointed at a boxy black vehicle about a dozen cars ahead. "That's them!"

"I think you're right," said Tesla. "Quick, Uncle Newt, get closer!"

Uncle Newt flapped a hand at the cars zipping down the hill into town. "I can't. This is a no passing lane, and there's too much traffic coming in the opposite direction."

"Try to get Agent McIntyre's attention," said Nick. "The Newtmobile is pretty distinctive. If she looks back, she'll know it's us."

"Good thinking!" Tesla cried, patting her brother on the arm (though in her excitement, it was more

147

like pounding), exactly where she'd whacked him a minute before. "Let's make some noise!"

Uncle Newt began honking the horn and flashing the headlights. It was impossible to tell if Agent McIntyre noticed, but plenty of other drivers certainly did. They honked back, flashed their own lights, and even made a few rude gestures.

"I guess they think I'm complaining about the traffic," Uncle Newt said.

"That doesn't matter," said Tesla. "Keep it up!"

Uncle Newt went on blasting the horn and flashing the lights, and Nick and Tesla stood in the backseat and began waving their hands over their heads.

"Agent McIntyre! It's us! Tesla and Nick!" shouted Tesla.

"Look back! Look back!" shouted Nick. "Don't you ever use your rearview mirror? *Look back!*"

Unfortunately, at that very moment the road ahead curved to the left, and the SUV rounded the bend and disappeared from sight.

Even more unfortunately, a California Highway Patrol motorcycle started following the Newtmobile, with siren howling.

"Oh, great," Nick moaned. "Just what we need."

"Don't be so pessimistic," said Tesla. "This might be *exactly* what we need."

Just as they reached a roadside antiques store on the right, Uncle Newt pulled into the gravel parking lot and stopped. The police officer did the same.

The officer set the kickstand on his motorcycle, spoke on his radio for a moment, and then approached the Newtmobile with slow, swaggering steps. The expression on his lean face was unreadable, his eyes hidden behind a pair of jet-black sunglasses.

"You've got to help us, Officer," Tesla said as he

stepped up to the car.

The officer's emotionless face did not change. He merely pointed his head in Tesla's direction.

Undeterred, she took that as a cue to keep talking.

"We were chasing an SUV that has a government agent in it—we don't know who specifically she works for, but it's got to be the CIA or something like that—because we just found out that her partner is working for a group of spies that's been trying to steal our parents' work on space-based solar-power transmission, and if we don't warn her, he's probably going to sabotage it when she tries to trace the spies using the hacked laptop we just gave her and . . . and . . . You don't believe a word of this, do you?"

The policeman didn't even bother to reply. He just turned his stony, blank expression to Uncle Newt and said:

"License and registration."

Uncle Newt was cited for reckless driving, improper use of signals, and having un-seat-belted minors in a moving vehicle. (Nick and Tesla had removed their seatbelts in order to stand and wave in their failed attempt to attract Agent McIntyre's attention.) He was also warned that the Newtmobile needed heavy-duty vehicle certification and a smog check. After all that, they were finally allowed to go on their way.

The ticketing process had taken twenty minutes, so it was no use trying to catch up to the SUV. Agents McIntyre and Doyle were long gone.

Uncle Newt turned the Newtmobile around and headed back toward Half Moon Bay.

"The FBI must have a local office in San Francisco," Uncle Newt said. "When we get home, we'll call them."

"They'll probably believe us as much as that cop did," Nick grumbled.

Tesla gave him another swat. "Hey, it's worth a try," she said. "We can call the CIA, too."

"And the Pentagon, and the National Security Agency," added Uncle Newt. "The worst they can do is hang up on us, right?"

"Right," Tesla agreed. "In the meantime, Agent McIntyre will have someone working on that laptop.

Maybe they'll be able to trace the hack to the bad guys."

Nick shook his head. "The laptop's probably useless now. Doyle warned Control about it, remember? They'll have plenty of time to cover their tracks. And while they're doing that, they'll also be getting ready for Option A that Doyle mentioned on the phone. Whatever that is, I don't think it'll be good news for us, or Mom and Dad."

"We don't know anything for sure," said Tesla—though she suspected that, for once, her brother's worst-case scenario was pretty close to accurate.

Uncle Newt seemed to be thinking the same thing.

No one spoke another word during the entire trip home.

When they reached Uncle Newt's house, Mr. Kuskie's blue VW Rabbit was no longer out front. Even more surprisingly, Silas and DeMarco were gone, too.

"I would've thought they'd wait around to see how the car chase turned out," said Tesla.

"We left the doors to the house unlocked," Nick pointed out. "Maybe they're inside."

That's exactly where they were.

And they weren't alone.

When Nick, Tesla, and Uncle Newt walked into the dining room, they found their friends lying on the floor, hands bound behind their backs, ankles tied together, mouths gagged. Standing near them were three women, one with short dark hair, the other two with identical gray perms.

Nick and Tesla remembered the three intruders well. The last time they'd seen them, it was the women who had been the prisoners.

That had been the day Agent McIntyre drove off with Julie Casserly, the next-door-neighbor spy, and her deceptively decrepit-looking lackeys, Ethel and Gladys—who dressed and looked like sweet old grannies but in fact were trained to fight like ruthless ninjas.

And now they were back.

"Hello, again," Julie said as the women quickly fanned out, each one blocking an exit. "Miss me?"

Uncle Newt seemed to think over her question. "No," he answered finally. "Not particularly."

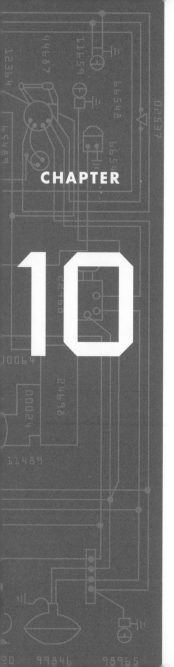

Nick and Tesla and Uncle Newt tried to resist, but there was no time for them to whip up a clever scheme or ingenious gadget to save themselves. They had to defend themselves—and it was soon obvious who were the professionals when it came to fighting: Julie and Ethel and Gladys.

The women grabbed wrists, twisted arms, swept feet off the floor with lightning-quick kicks. Within seconds, they had Nick, Tesla, and Uncle Newt pinned, bound, and gagged.

"We should have done this a

long time ago," Julie said with a smirk, gazing down on her prisoners. She dusted off her hands and then turned to Ethel and Gladys. "Bring up the truck."

Without a word, the gray-haired accomplices stalked out of the house. When they returned a moment later, between them they carried what appeared to be a rolled-up rug.

Nick and Tesla looked at each other.

Chuh? said the look in Nick's eyes.

Tesla could only shrug.

"The big dopey one first," said Julie.

"Which big dopey one?" Ethel (or maybe Gladys) asked.

Julie pointed at Uncle Newt.

"Him. The grown-up."

"HMPH URMMPH!" Uncle Newt muffled into his gag.

Julie chuckled. "Please, watch your language. There are children present," she said.

Ethel and Gladys dropped the rug next to Uncle Newt, rolled it out, and pushed him onto it. They then proceeded to wrap him up in it like a pig in a blanket.

"HMPH URMMPH!" he said again, but the words

were even more muffled this time, and no one bothered to reply as Ethel and Gladys lifted him up and lugged his squirmy body through the kitchen.

The old women returned carrying only the rug. They repeated the operation with Tesla, then Nick, then Silas, then DeMarco.

Once everyone had been unceremoniously dumped into the back of a small moving truck that was now parked in the driveway, Julie came out to inspect Ethel and Gladys's handiwork (as the panting, visibly overexerted women glared at her).

"You may as well get comfortable," Julie told her prisoners. "It's going to be a long, bumpy ride."

Then she reached up, grabbed the strap hanging from the bottom of the steel door, and yanked it down.

The door slammed shut with a deafening *clang*, sealing Nick and Tesla and the others in complete and utter darkness.

Julie Casserly was right about the long, bumpy ride. What she hadn't mentioned was how hot it was going to get.

Despite the total lack of light, the back of the truck didn't stay cool long. Tesla could feel the air growing warmer and staler by the minute, and soon her clothes were soaked with sweat.

It was also growing harder to breathe through the gag.

She rolled over on her side—it was impossible to lie comfortably on her back with her hands tied behind her—and tried to speak.

"How's everyone doing?" she asked.

It came out sounding like "Hurr wurwurwur wuhwuh?"

No one replied.

But Tesla heard movement, and a second later she felt a sudden, uncomfortable pressure weighing down on her. It seemed like someone was trying to sit on her, and she began to squirm away—until she realized what that someone was really trying to do.

Somebody was groping for her gag in the darkness.

Whoever it was, it couldn't have been Silas. She would have already been crushed to death.

Tesla stopped struggling, and the fumbling

fingers found her gag and yanked the cloth out of her mouth.

"Thank you!" Tesla gasped.

After sucking in a few deep breaths, she pressed her back into whoever had just helped her and began searching for a gag with her bound hands. After sticking her fingers into an ear, an eye, and a nostril, she finally found a mouth and pulled out the cloth stuffed within it.

The first thing Nick said was "Ouch." After catching his breath, he added, "But thanks."

"All right, Uncle Newt, Silas, DeMarco," Tesla said. "Let us know where you are, and Nick and I will get your gags out."

Tesla heard grunting and banging on the truck's metal floor.

"OK, OK," Nick said. "Here we come."

He rolled off into the darkness. Tesla tried to angle her body in a different direction and went rolling off as well.

What followed was like the most uncomfortable game of Twister ever played. There was lots of writhing and flailing and poking people in the eye. But eventually everyone was able to speak and breathe freely.

"Where do you think they're taking us?" DeMarco said.

"I don't know," replied Uncle Newt. "But they wouldn't have taken us prisoner if they didn't need us for some reason. And that means they aren't going to hurt us."

"For now," muttered Nick.

Tesla launched an awkward kick into the darkness toward the sound of her brother's voice. (It's hard to be graceful when your ankles are tied together.) It felt like she connected with one of his shins.

"Ow!" Nick yipped.

"Keep it positive," Tesla said.

"Gee, thanks for the reminder, Tez," Nick said. "Physical abuse is *just* what I need to improve my attitude."

"So," Silas began, "did you guys catch up to Agent McIntyre and tell her that Agent Doyle's a muskrat?"

Tesla silently cursed herself for not leaving Silas gagged when she had the chance.

"Excuse me?" said Uncle Newt.

"Did you tell Agent McIntyre that Agent Doyle's

a muskrat?" Silas said. "You know, a double agent."

Tesla heard her brother heave a long-suffering sigh. This time she let his negative attitude slide. "You mean a mole, Silas," Nick said. "And no. If we'd been able to tell her about Agent Doyle, we wouldn't be here right now, would we?"

"How did you and DeMarco get caught, anyway?" Tesla asked.

"I was kinda mad at my dad, so I told him he could just go," Silas said. "After he left, we decided to wait for you guys in Uncle Newt's kitchen."

"There's usually Coke in the fridge," DeMarco said, by way of explanation.

"Oooh. Ice-cold Coke," Silas moaned.

There was a smacking sound—Silas licking his parched lips, apparently—then he continued his story.

"So there we were sipping our Cokes, minding our own business, and all of a sudden BAMMO! Julie Casserly and her granny goons come bustin' in. We put up a pretty good fight, but they outnumbered us."

"By 'put up a pretty good fight,' he means we managed to throw our Cokes at them before they slammed us to the floor and tied us up," DeMarco said.

"Hey, that *is* putting up a pretty good fight!" Silas shot back. "Those old ladies are tough!"

"*Anyway*," said DeMarco. "Now what?"

"I guess we should see if we can get our hands and feet free," Nick said.

"That's more like it!" said Tesla.

She stretched a foot toward her brother's voice and ended up kicking him in the ear.

"Ow!"

"Sorry. That was supposed to be an approving pat on the shoulder."

"Well, maybe you should hold off until you can do it with your *hand*."

"Right."

Tesla began struggling against the straps that Julie and her minions had wrapped around her wrists and ankles. She heard her brother and the others doing the same.

"These aren't regular handcuffs," Silas grunted.

"Yeah. They're not metal," said DeMarco. "They feel more like plastic."

"Injection-molded nylon," said Uncle Newt. "A lot

of police departments use them these days. The military, too. They're lighter than metal, and there's no key to keep track of. When you're ready to set your prisoner free, you just cut the nylon off. Do any of you kids have a pocket knife?"

All four said no.

"Really?" said Uncle Newt, flabbergasted. "No one carries a Swiss Army knife anymore?"

"My mom barely trusts me with a spoon," said Silas.

"How about dental floss?" asked Uncle Newt.

Again, the kids all said no. "I must've left mine in my other pants," DeMarco added sarcastically.

"Seems like a weird time to floss," Silas whispered. "You think the heat's getting to him?"

"I see what you're thinking, Uncle Newt," Nick said. "You want us to use—"

"Friction!" Tesla broke in. "If you can *cut* through the nylon, then you can *saw* through it, too!"

"Exactly," said Uncle Newt. "If we had something long and thin, we could use it like a wire saw. It wouldn't have to be as strong as the nylon—just strong enough to stay in one piece as the friction between it and the nylon creates heat energy."

"A belt!" Silas suggested.

"Not thin enough," said Uncle Newt.

"Hair!" Silas suggested.

"Not thick enough," said Uncle Newt.

"Shoelaces!" Silas suggested.

"Not . . ." Uncle Newt's voice trailed off. Then, after a long silence he said, "You know what? That might just work. Can anyone get Silas's shoelaces off?"

"Oh, I don't have laces on my shoes," Silas said. "I only wear Vans slip-ons."

Tesla heard her brother sigh again. "My shoes have laces," she said.

"Mine, too," said DeMarco.

"And mine," said Nick.

"And mine, so we've got plenty to work with," said Uncle Newt. "Let's get to it!"

Another round of blind Twister followed, with everybody fumbling in the dark for one another's shoes and struggling to untie the laces, sight unseen. Every so often the truck would hit a bump or turn sharply, and the imprisoned passengers would go bouncing across the metal floor and lose their place. Then, covered in new bruises they couldn't even see, they had to refind one another's feet and pick up where they'd left off.

It was slow, exhausting work, but eventually they all had shoelaces in their bound hands.

Then began the even slower, even more exhausting work of using the laces to free their hands and feet.

Two shoelaces broke as Nick tried to saw through his uncle's restraints. Silas lost a couple more when a particularly big bump sent him flying.

But then DeMarco said, "I think it's working!" as he awkwardly sawed at the restraints around Tesla's wrists, his back to hers. A minute later, Tesla felt her hands pop free.

The process got a lot easier after that.

Tesla freed DeMarco's hands, together they freed Uncle Newt and Nick and Silas's hands, and then everybody started working to free their own feet. Eventually, all the laces but one had been torn apart by the friction and heat. But by that point one shoelace was all they needed.

The restraints around Silas's ankles were the last to go.

Everyone was free.

"All right!" DeMarco said. "Now we can . . . umm . . . what *are* we going to do now?"

"I say when they open the back door, we jump them," said Tesla. "It'll be five against three. I think we can take them."

"I say when they open the back door, we run for it," said Nick. "They can't catch us all. One of us will be able to get away and alert the authorities."

"You know," Silas said dreamily, "I've always wanted to alert the authorities about something. Besides alerting my dad that his car's engine is on fire again."

Everyone ignored him.

"What do you think, Uncle Newt?" Nick asked.

"I don't know, Nick. Is there a way we can fight *and* run away?"

"Not really," said Tesla.

"Yeah, I don't think so," said Nick.

"OK. Well. Gosh. I guess as the adult here I should be more decisive, but . . . anyone have a coin we could flip?"

"How would we see it?" DeMarco asked.

"Oh. Good point."

Suddenly a piercing metallic screech sounded beneath their feet—squealing brakes—and they all began rolling and sliding toward the front of the truck. A moment later, as they wriggled out of the heap they'd ended up in, Tesla pressed a palm against the floor.

For the first time since they left Half Moon Bay, it wasn't vibrating.

"We've stopped," Tesla said. "And I think they turned the engine off."

"We're here . . . wherever 'here' is," Nick said softly.

"Time to decide," said DeMarco. "What are we going to do?"

"We're going to fight," Uncle Newt announced. Tesla heard him stand up and walk toward the big metal door at the back of the truck. "And *then* run away if that doesn't work. Who's with me?"

Tesla pushed herself up and walked through the darkness to stand beside her uncle.

"Me," she said.

She heard somebody step up beside her.

"And me," said Nick. "I guess . . ."

More footsteps.

"And me," said DeMarco.

Yet more footsteps echoed through the blackness—followed by a dull thud as someone walked into the side of the truck.

"Oof," said Silas. "And me."

"We're over here," DeMarco whispered.

Silas shuffled over to join the others.

"All right, kids," Uncle Newt said. "The second they open that door, we're going to AHHHHHHHH!"

Before he could finish his sentence, someone was opening the door—and fast. It rattled loudly as it slid and rolled up like a garage door, flooding the back of the truck with light.

Nick, Tesla, Silas, and DeMarco each did a version of Uncle Newt's "AHHHHHHHH!" All five of them spun around and backed away, their hands pressed over their faces. They hadn't realized what a sudden burst of bright light would feel like after spending so long in total darkness. The sun streaming into their eyes was very, very bright indeed. Blindingly bright. Literally.

They couldn't fight. They couldn't even run. All

they could do was shield their eyes and wipe away tears and wait for their vision to return to normal.

"What have you done to them?" a woman's anguished voice asked.

Tesla turned toward the voice—toward the blinding light—despite the new pain it brought her already hurting eyes.

"They'd better not be harmed," a man's voice said sternly.

Tesla heard someone else spin around beside her. She knew it had to be Nick.

Tesla blinked into the light and swiped away more tears; as she did so, the blank whiteness before her eyes began to fade. After a few more seconds, she was at last able to look into the bright opening of the back of the truck and, just beyond it, could see five hazy shapes.

Five people.

Two of the people immediately pulled themselves up into the truck and quickly walked—no, practically ran—the few steps to reach Nick and Tesla. These were the people whose voices Tesla and Nick had recognized: a plump woman with short blonde hair and cat's-eye glasses and a tall, slender man with a neatly trimmed beard and a ponytail.

"Mom?" said Nick.

"Dad?" said Tesla.

"Yes," said their father.

"We're here," said their mother.

Nick and Tesla bolted forward and threw themselves into their parents' arms.

The pain in Tesla's eyes was gone now, but her tears were flowing faster than ever.

Tesla was hugging her dad. Nick was hugging his mom. Then Uncle Newt's long arms encircled them all, and suddenly it was a big group hug.

"Al! Martha!" Uncle Newt said. "We didn't know if we'd ever see you again!"

After a few more seconds, yet another pair of arms wrapped themselves around the family and squeezed hard. A little too hard, actually.

The five Holts turned to look at Silas, who was bear-hugging them with all his might.

"Sorry," he said, reluctantly letting go. "I just couldn't resist."

"All right, all right—that's enough touchy-feely." Julie Casserly's sardonic voice broke up the happy reunion. "Come on, get out." Nick and Tesla saw their nemesis standing outside the truck, along with her aging lackeys.

"I said come out," Julie snapped. "Or else *they* come in." She poked a thumb at Ethel and Gladys.

The old women grinned malevolently and cracked their ancient knuckles. The kids knew from experience that the threat was real.

"We're coming," Tesla said hurriedly.

She and the rest of the prisoners did as they were told, hopping out of the truck one by one. Nick and Tesla and their parents moved almost as a single unit, keeping close and separating only briefly as they jumped onto the ground.

"Whoa," Silas said, taking in their surroundings.

The truck was parked in front of a large, dilapidated gray building. Nearby were other buildings—smaller but just as ramshackle—and what looked like abandoned airplane hangars. In the distance were a guard tower and a chain-link fence and, stretching around them all the way to the horizon, an immense, flat, featureless desert.

Wherever they were, one thing was obvious: it was the middle of nowhere.

"What is this place?" Tesla asked.

"We're—" Mr. Holt started to explain, but then stopped short.

He threw Julie a questioning glance.

"Go ahead—tell them," she said with an indifferent shrug. "It doesn't matter now."

Mr. Holt looked back to the kids and Uncle Newt.

"We're in the Great Basin Desert," he said. "At Brace Air Force Base."

DeMarco glanced around at the decaying buildings, the empty sky, the pothole-pocked road that stretched straight west for miles and miles without a car in sight.

"This is an air force base?"

"It's been closed for years," Mr. Holt explained.

"How long have you been here?" Nick asked.

"Me? About a week."

"They brought me here only yesterday," said Mrs. Holt. "Until you found that office in Mountain View, they had us working on separate control systems for the—"

"OK, that's enough," Julie interrupted.

"You said it didn't matter what they tell us now," Tesla said.

Julie sneered at her. "It doesn't. But Control will probably want to tell you that part of the story."

"Control is here?" Nick asked.

Julie nodded at the big gray building. "Right in there. Waiting. Now let's go."

Ethel and Gladys stepped forward to give the nearest prisoners—Silas and Uncle Newt—a hard shove.

"No need to get pushy!" Tesla snapped at them. "We get the idea."

She and the others headed toward the building. As she climbed the crumbling concrete steps, Tesla could make out sun-bleached words barely visible over the entrance.

BRACE A.F.B. AIR DEFENSE COMMAND
HOME OF THE 52nd AIR DIVISION

The group entered a large, empty lobby and turned left. Mr. and Mrs. Holt led the way down a dark corridor, each keeping an arm around the twins nearly the whole way. Ethel, Gladys, and Julie brought up the rear.

"In here," Mrs. Holt said when they reached an open door halfway down the hall.

They all filed into what looked like the Mission Control room that had handled a moon shot circa 1969—and that hadn't been used, or cleaned, ever since. Rows of workstations were covered with clunky electronic panels and old-fashioned phones and desk chairs on wheels and lots and *lots* of dust.

At the far end of the room, a person was sitting in a black tall-backed chair at one of the workstations. Several nearby TV monitors, set into the walls and panels, were active. One showed a reporter standing in front of the White House, the words WORLD LEADERS GATHER TO RENEW "STAR WARS" BAN on the screen underneath her. Another screen displayed a familiar coastline half-covered with clouds—the East Coast of North America, viewed from space.

The person in the chair began to chortle. Then laugh. Then cackle demonically:

"Bwa-ha-ha-ha-ha-haaa! BWA-HA-HA-HA-HA-HAAAAAAAA!"

The chair spun around, revealing not only the man seated in it but also the images on the screen in front of him.

He'd been watching an episode of *The Simpsons*.

At last, he noticed that he wasn't alone.

"Oh. You're here," he said, his guffaws ceasing instantly. "Sorry, that show always cracks me up."

The man in the chair was short, pudgy, and balding. He seemed to be in his late forties or early fifties, and he was dressed in a bright Hawaiian shirt, cargo shorts, and sandals.

He spread his arms in a welcoming gesture.

"Have a seat, everybody. Who wants Kool-Aid and cookies?"

DeMarco and Silas both said "Me!" as they sat down in the nearest chairs.

With their parents and uncle standing behind them, Nick and Tesla stayed on their feet, motionless, their stunned stares locked onto the little man.

"*You?*" said Tesla in disbelief.

"*You're* Control?" said Nick.

The man grinned. "Oh, there's no need for coy code names now," he said. "Call me Bob."

"*Bob?*" said Nick.

The man nodded, still grinning.

"The person who's been hounding our parents and spying on us and trying to steal government secrets?" Tesla said.

Bob's grin faded slightly. "Well," he said, his voice a nasal whine, "I suppose you could look at it that way."

"The man who broke up our family and terrorized us and had us kidnapped?" Tesla continued. "And you want us to call you *Bob*?"

"Control was cooler," DeMarco pointed out.

"And Sun King was *way* cooler," added Silas. He

pointed a finger at DeMarco and made a *pshew* laser noise.

DeMarco spun his chair, leaned toward his friend, and dropped his voice to a whisper (although everyone in the room could still hear it). "I don't think this guy's got the pizzazz to pull off Sun King."

"Oh, I don't know," Silas "whispered" back. "Maybe if he lost a little weight and hid his bald spot under a helmet and put on a cape and . . ." He squinted at the man and then shrugged. "Yeah, you're right. He's much more of a Bob."

As Silas and DeMarco debated, Tesla took a step toward Bob, her right fist clinched.

"I know a better name for you than Control or Bob," she said. She took another step forward. "It's lousy, stinking, no-good—"

Ethel (or maybe it was Gladys) moved quickly to block Tesla's path. In her wrinkly hands was a plate of cookies.

"Have an Oreo," she snarled, her face an ominous scowl. "They're the extra-creamy kind."

Tesla and the old woman glared at each other until Silas popped between them to fill his hands with cookies.

"Oooo! Double Stuf!" he said. "My mom never buys these!"

Tesla felt a hand on her shoulder, and she glanced behind to find her father backing her up gently.

"You didn't drag them out here for a picnic, *Bob*," he said, his usually soft voice as steely as Tesla had ever heard it. "Cut out the small talk and get to the point."

Bob heaved a sigh and slumped a little lower in his seat. He looked like his feelings were genuinely hurt. "All right," he said. "The point."

He focused his gaze on Nick, and his smile returned. The sight of it was so creepy that Mrs. Holt quickly stepped closer behind her son and draped her arms around his shoulders as if to protect him.

"I know all about you, Nick," Bob said. "You're the reasonable one. The one who worries about being prudent. Staying safe."

Nick knew that was true but couldn't help feel insulted. "Maybe," he admitted reluctantly.

"You want your country to be safe, right, Nick?" Bob asked.

Nick shrugged. "I guess."

Bob's smile broadened. "Then you should be glad

you're here. Because keeping your country safe is what this project is all about."

"I get the feeling my mom and dad wouldn't agree with you about that," Nick said.

"Or the government," said Tesla.

"True," Bob conceded. "There has been a little disagreement over how to use a certain piece of technology."

Tesla impatiently rolled her hands in the air. "Yeah, yeah—the space-based solar-power system. We know all about that."

"You do?" Mrs. Holt blurted out in surprise. Mr. Holt looked shocked, too.

"We guessed it a while ago," Nick said. "Once we knew that spies were chasing you, it became pretty obvious you guys weren't really soybean experts."

"You've been lying to us our whole lives about what you do, haven't you?" Tesla said. She stepped away from her father and turned to him accusingly. "I bet that's even why you gave us our names. You were working on a wireless energy transmission system, and Nikola Tesla was the first scientist to seriously try to build one."

Over at their workstation, Silas leaned in and elbowed DeMarco in the ribs. "This is getting juicy," he whispered, popping another cookie into his mouth.

"Yes, honey, we did lie to you," Mr. Holt said. "And I'm sorry about that. But the project had to stay completely secret."

"So you lied to your own kids?" Tesla said. "Didn't tell them the truth about who you really are?"

Nick moved away from his mother to stand next to Tesla. "You should have trusted us," he said. "Who would we have told your secrets to, anyway? It's not like we were having play dates with Russian spies."

Mr. and Mrs. Holt exchanged a sad, guilty look, then turned back to their children. "Kids," their father said, "you're the most important people in the world to us. We love you and trust you. But this was just too big for you to know about. You're *children*."

Nick and Tesla stiffened.

"We had to take every precaution to protect you," Mrs. Holt added. "There was simply too much danger that the technology would be misused."

Bob interrupted by blowing a raspberry.

"You know what would be a *real* misuse of that satellite?" he said. "Beaming free power to all the gimme-gimme moochers of the world." He turned to Nick again and jerked his thumb at the boy's parents. "That's what those two wanted to do. When instead you could up the frequency of the beam the teeniest bit and have—"

"A weapon," Tesla cut in. "We already guessed that, too."

Bob shook his head. "Not a weapon. A proactive defense system."

"A weapon," Tesla repeated.

Bob continued to shake his head. "A proactive defense system."

"A *weapon*."

"A *proactive defense system*."

"Bob," Mrs. Holt said, "your plan is to fry people from space."

Bob threw his hands up in the air. "Fine! A *weapon!* Weapon, weapon, WEAPON!" he roared, a string of spittle flying halfway across the room. He looked as if he might pop out of his seat and fly across the room, too. "Whatever! The point is, we'd have it and the other guys wouldn't!"

A moment of silence followed during which everyone else in the room—even Julie and Gladys and Ethel—stared at Bob warily while he wiped saliva from the front of his Hawaiian shirt.

"Now *that* was almost over-the-top enough for 'Sun King,'" Silas whispered to DeMarco through a mouthful of Oreos.

Uncle Newt, who had been standing quietly next to his brother and taking everything in, now stepped forward and addressed Bob directly. "Who is this 'we'? Who are these 'other guys'?" His voice was quiet yet firm. "And—most important of all—*who are you?*"

"He used to be our boss, Newt, before we started at the National Science Foundation," said Mr. Holt.

"That's who we really work for," Mrs. Holt said to Nick and Tesla. "Not the Department of Agriculture."

"We found out a few months ago that he and some of his cronies were planning to weaponize our work, in violation of government policy," Mr. Holt added.

Uncle Newt nodded at the bank of TV screens near Bob. "And international law," he said. On the monitor that was tuned to a news network, the U.S. president could be seen standing at a podium speaking. Across the bottom of the screen were the words PRESIDENT ANSWERS QUESTIONS AS TREATY

SIGNING NEARS.

Bob rolled his eyes. "Government policy? International law? Who cares about those?"

"See what we mean?" Mr. Holt said. "We went to the National Science Foundation's inspector general with what we'd learned, and she brought in the FBI," Mrs. Holt said. "But Bob got wind of the investigation and tried to have us kidnapped. That's when we went on the run. It wasn't supposed to be for long—just until Agent McIntyre could capture Bob and the others. But eventually we were captured instead. The conspiracy was bigger than we thought."

Silas snapped his fingers, sending cookie crumbs flying. "Agent Doyle!" he said, clearly pleased with himself for being able to follow the Holts' story. "The traitor!"

Bob sat up straight, his round face flushed suddenly. "Did you just call us . . . traitors?" he snarled.

Mr. and Mrs. Holt, Ethel, Gladys, and Julie all froze, faces pale, eyes wide. They looked as if a tiger had just sauntered into the room, and they were hoping he'd saunter right out again if they stood stock still and stayed quiet.

"Don't use the T-word around Bob," Mrs. Holt

said to Silas.

"What?" said Silas. "You mean 'traitor'?"

Mr. and Mrs. Holt winced.

Bob hopped up out of his chair. "Who's a traitor?" he barked at Silas.

"Agent Doyle," Silas said.

"Oh, really?" Bob snapped back. "And who does Doyle work for?"

"Uhh . . . you?"

"Yes! That's right! And if Doyle is a traitor, what does that make the man who controls him?"

"Well . . ."

DeMarco nudged Silas. "Don't say it," he said under his breath.

". . . I guess he'd be a . . ."

"*Don't say it, Silas*," DeMarco hissed.

". . . a . . . T-word?" Silas finished.

In that instant, Bob's face changed from pink to nearly purple. He charged toward Silas and DeMarco and grabbed the Oreos piled on the electronic panel between them.

"NO! COOKIES! FOR! YOU!" he bellowed, crushing the Oreos in his hands. "I AM NOT A T-WORD! I AM A P-WORD! A PATRIOT!"

Bob pelted Silas and DeMarco with bits of crushed cookie and then, as the boys ducked under the workstation they'd been sitting at, stomped toward the TV screens.

"You want to see traitors?" Bob roared. "These are the traitors!"

Silas poked his head up and squinted at the screens. "The Simpsons?" he said.

Bob screamed incoherently and stomped over to Gladys (or maybe it was Ethel) in search of more cookies to throw. He grabbed two fistfuls and spun around toward Silas.

Tesla jumped between Bob and her friend, and Nick hurried over to stand by her side.

"We get it, Bob! We get it!" Tesla said, putting up her hands.

"The people in Washington are the . . . the you-know-whats," said Nick.

Bob glared at them a moment, panting heavily. Then he slammed the Oreos back onto the plate that Gladys/Ethel was holding. The old woman looked relieved that he didn't throw them at *her*.

"Oh, they're you-know-whats, all right," Bob said with a sneer. Slowly, with each wheezing breath, his flushed face faded to its previous pasty, pale complexion. "In two days," he said, "they're going to sign a treaty that would force us to give up the greatest edge we've ever had over our enemies . . . all in the name of peace and international goodwill."

Bob said "peace and international goodwill" the way some people would say "cockroaches and rats." He dusted crumbs off his hands and then continued his rant.

"I'm not going to let them do it. In orbit over this planet is a satellite that your parents helped design and build. An operational prototype for a space-based microwave-power transmitter." The creepy smile slowly returned to Bob's puffy face. "I've seen the demonstrations. I know what it's capable of, and what it is capable of doing with just a few minor adjustments. Adjustments your parents have been dragging their feet to make. But now I've brought them a helper: a brilliant scientist who used to work for the Jet Propulsion Laboratory."

"No one from JPL would help you," said Uncle Newt.

"He means you, Newt," Mr. Holt said, sighing.

"Oh." Uncle Newt folded his arms across his

chest and stared at Bob defiantly. "Well, I won't help you, either."

"Please, Dr. Holt. Think of the children," Bob said.

He stepped menacingly toward Nick and Tesla. Though they flinched at his approach, they managed to hold their ground.

Bob slipped behind them and placed his arms around their shoulders.

Mr. Holt stepped toward him, his face twisted with rage.

Julie stopped him simply by clearing her throat and nodding at Ethel and Gladys.

"Think about your niece and nephew's future," Bob was saying, "and what a shame it would be *if they didn't have one.*"

He gave Nick and Tesla a squeeze.

Uncle Newt wasn't confused this time. He knew exactly what Bob was saying—and that he meant it.

"You win," Uncle Newt said. "I'll do whatever you ask." Though he may have been giving in, Uncle Newt didn't look defeated. On the contrary, his eyes were blazing with an indignation and contempt the likes of which Nick and Tesla had never seen.

Bob seemed amused. "Good," he said, grinning.

"*You* can have all the cookies you want."

Nick and Tesla squirmed out of the man's grasp.

"Uncle Newt, you can't!" said Tesla.

"Mom, Dad—don't help him!" said Nick. "He's crazy!"

Bob's smile disappeared again. Apparently he didn't like that word, either.

"Family-reunion time's over," he said coldly. "Julie, show our young *guests* to their room. And be sure they know what will happen to them if they leave it."

Julie nodded and stepped out of the doorway.

"Come on," she said, jerking her head at the hallway outside. "Let's go."

Silas and DeMarco trudged toward the door.

Nick and Tesla started to follow but then simultaneously swerved to their parents and threw their arms around them.

"Don't worry," Mr. Holt said reassuringly as he and his wife hugged them back. "Everything's going to be all right."

"We know," said Tesla.

"We'll get you out of this," Nick said quietly.

Mr. and Mrs. Holt both blinked at their children

in surprise. These weren't the same scared, confused kids they'd sent to live with their Uncle Newt. They had changed.

Tesla squeezed her parents even harder. "We're still mad at you, though," she added.

"That's enough of that," said Ethel (or was it Gladys?).

"Break it up," added Gladys (or was it Ethel?).

The old women pulled the family apart and pushed Nick and Tesla toward the door.

"All right—no more distractions, no more delays, no more excuses," the kids heard Bob say as Julie marched them away. "I want my *weapon*!"

Julie marched her prisoners through a series of long, gloomy hallways to a room at the back of the building. It appeared to have been used most recently as a workshop: scattered on old metal desks was an assortment of electronic equipment and circuit boards and tools. Through the single narrow window, the kids could see the base's airfield and, beyond it, the flat expanse of desert.

Long, deep shadows stretched away from the side of the building. The sun was beginning to set.

Julie nodded at the window. "Do you know what's out there?"

"Nothing?" DeMarco guessed, squinting at the yellow featureless landscape outside.

Julie shook her head. "Not quite. There's thirty miles of wasteland in all directions. That's something. And there's sun and snakes and coyotes. That's something, too. Which is why, if you go out there, we might not even bother coming after you. Because you'll be toast within half a day without any help from us. Got it?"

"Got it," DeMarco said, nodding solemnly.

Julie spun on her heel and strode out of the room, closing and locking the door behind her.

The kids just stood rooted to the ground for a moment, listening as her footsteps faded away down the hall.

"So," DeMarco said when it was quiet again, "what's the plan?"

Nick and Tesla were already moving around the room, inspecting the tools and equipment.

"We're working on it," Tesla said.

Silas went to the window and started fiddling with a handle attached to the frame. At first it wouldn't budge, but eventually he was able to turn it. He jerked on it, and with a rusty squeal, the bottom half of the window opened inward a few inches.

"Hey!" Silas said. "I might be able to get this open far enough for us to climb out!"

"And then what?" DeMarco said.

Silas kept tugging on the window. It was open about half a foot now.

"Then we steal the truck, ram into the side of the building, rescue the grown-ups, and escape."

"How do we get the keys?" Nick asked as he rummaged through a garbage can full of discarded wires, cables, and circuits (and popsicle sticks, juice bottles, and candy bar wrappers). "And how do we know where to ram into the building? And even if we can break through the wall, how do we know we won't run over my mom and dad or Uncle Newt? And do any of us even know how to drive? And—"

"All right, all right!" Silas said. "Maybe it's not the best plan in the world! I'm just spitballing here, OK?"

Tesla leaned over the bin Nick was looking through and fished out a flat black rectangle about the size of a playing card. Nick reached in and pulled out two more.

Solar panels!

"Bob must have had Mom and Dad in here working on something," Tesla said. "If we can find the right piece of equipment in their leftovers—"

"Like this maybe?" Nick said, lifting out two plastic bottles and tilting them to show off the lids.

Tesla grinned.

"*Exactly* like that," she said.

Silas and DeMarco turned to look at the trash their friends found so fascinating. "How is that junk gonna help us?" DeMarco asked.

"Maybe we can't make it thirty miles through the desert to get help," Nick said. "But what if someone else— "

"Or some*thing* else," Tesla added.

"—did it for us?"

SOLAR-POWERED
LONG-RANGE ROVER

THE STUFF

- 3-volt DC motor

- 2 AA 1.5-volt rechargeable batteries and battery holder

- A 1.5-watt solar panel

- 2 popsicle sticks

- 4 12-inch bamboo skewers

- 4 large bottle caps (the kind on juice bottles)

- A plastic deli-container lid

- 3 NTE578 Schottky diodes

- A nail

- Cardboard scraps

- 1 plastic straw

- Wire cutters

- A hot-glue gun

- Double-sided tape

- Scissors

- A drill (optional)

MAKE THE CAR FRAME

1. Cut out 3 1-by-1.5-inch (2 by 3 cm) pieces of cardboard and glue them together in a stack. Glue 2 popsicle sticks on top, lengthwise, with equal lengths of the sticks sticking out on either side of the stack. Trim the straw to about the same length as the popsicle sticks and glue it on top.

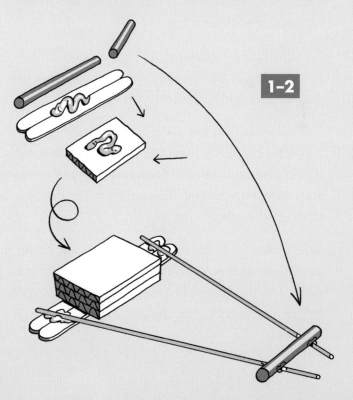

1–2

2. Trim the pointed ends off 2 skewers. Position them as shown on page 195, forming a triangle, and glue the cut end of the straw on top of the skewers at the narrow end. Flip over the cardboard stack and glue the wide end of the skewers on top of the popsicle sticks.

ATTACH THE WHEELS

3. Using a nail or drill (and the help of a responsible adult, if you need it), make a hole as wide as a bamboo skewer in the center of each bottle cap.

4. Cut a third skewer to a length about 5 inches (12.5 cm). It should be longer than the wide end of the car frame, with room on each end for the bottle cap wheels.

5. Push the skewer into one of the bottle caps, with the open side of the cap facing inward. Glue the outside end of the skewer onto the wheel. Slip the skewer through the straw that's under the wide end of the car frame and then glue the other wheel in place.

6. Glue another bottle cap onto one end of the last skewer, then slip the skewer through the straw at the narrow end of the frame. Trim the skewer's free end so that it is just long enough to hold another bottle cap. Slip on the bottle cap and glue in place.

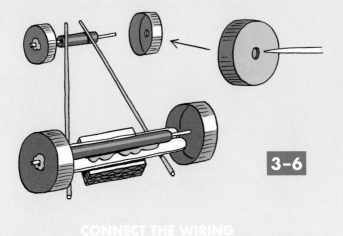

3-6

7. Line up 2 diodes with the stripes on the ends facing each other. Twist together the wires on the facing ends.

8. Connect the third diode to the first two as shown, with one wire twisted onto each of the free wires of diodes 1 and 2.

9. Attach the battery pack. Twist the red wire from the battery pack to the wire coming from the right end of the diodes (the end with the stripe on the upper diode). Attach the black wire from the battery pack to the motor.

10. Attach the solar panel. Twist the red wire from the solar panel to the wire coming from the left side of the diodes. Twist the black wire from the solar panel to the motor, on the same end where the battery pack is attached.

11. Attach the diodes. Use a length of extra wire to connect the free end of the motor to the connection between the two lower diodes. With batteries in the battery pack, the motor should spin. Remove the batteries, or disconnect one of the wires, to stop the motor.

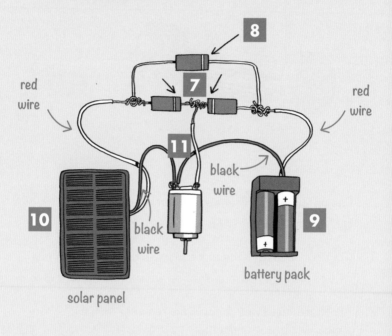

red wire

red wire

black wire

black wire

solar panel

battery pack

MAKE THE PROPELLER

12. Copy the fan pattern on page 261 onto a piece of paper. Then trace it onto the deli container lid and cut it out. Bend the blades as shown. The sides of the blades should be bent up and down in an alternating pattern: one up, the next one down, and so on.

13. Poke a hole in the center of the fan and slip it onto the shaft of the motor. Make sure it turns freely, and then glue it in place.

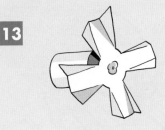

THE FINAL STEPS

1. Glue the motor onto the wide end of the cardboard frame. Make sure the fan turns freely before you glue it.

2. Glue a piece of cardboard across the middle of the frame, then glue the battery pack on top of that. Finally, glue the solar panel on top of the battery pack, tilted up and facing forward.

3. Add batteries to get the car rolling. The solar panel will recharge the batteries between rides. You can also run the car with the panel detached to get more speed (there will be less weight; just wire the battery directly to the motor). Experiment with bigger fans for more wind power! You can disconnect the batteries to see how the car moves on solar power alone. Can you find ways to make the car lighter so that it goes faster on solar energy?

1–3

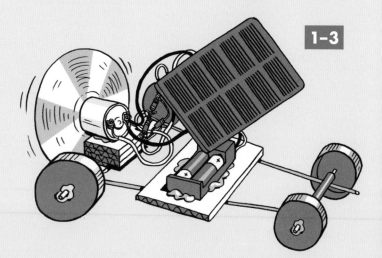

Nick and Tesla worked on the solar-powered rover for the next hour, trying out different combinations of sticks, wires, improvised wheels, and a miniature driver that Silas insisted they include (which they threw away as soon as his back was turned). Their only break came when their lookout by the door—DeMarco—reported hearing footsteps in the hall. Nick and Tesla quickly hid the tools while their lookout by the window—Silas—scrambled over to position in front of the half-finished rover.

The kids listened as someone

unlocked the door. Seconds later, Ethel and Gladys entered carrying ratty old sofa cushions and a bag of tortilla chips.

"Here's your bedding," one of them said as she dumped the cushions on the floor.

"And here's your dinner," the other one said, tossing the chips to Silas.

"Thanks," said Silas. "Got any salsa?"

"Or some carrots?" DeMarco asked loudly, drawing the old ladies' attention his way. "Not everyone's into junk food, you know."

Ethel and Gladys ignored their requests and stalked out of the room, locking the door behind them.

"Oh, well," Silas said as he tore open the bag of chips. "Fortunately, some of us *are* into junk food."

Nick and Tesla got right back to work.

Two hours later, they were done. Or so they hoped. The solar panels and batteries were feeding power to the rover's wheels, but it was barely enough to generate movement.

"I'd like to be rescued sometime this year, if possible," DeMarco said as he watched the rover inch across the floor with all the speed of a sleepwalking tortoise. "That thing's not gonna reach the highway for at least a decade."

"What's with the batteries?" Silas asked. "I thought this thing ran on sun power."

"Lots of solar power systems use batteries," Nick explained, "so that the energy collected from the sun can be stored and used when there's no sunlight."

"These batteries are rechargeable but weren't juiced up," Tesla said. She pointed up at the flickering old fluorescent lights hanging overhead. "And those things aren't bright enough to recharge them quickly. But when the sun comes out tomorrow morning, the batteries will charge and the rover will really get going."

"You sure about that?" DeMarco asked.

The rover, now in the shadow cast by one of the desks, was moving even more slowly than before. It was going about as fast as a sleepwalking tortoise with a sprained ankle.

"We're sure," said Nick somewhat unconvincingly. He was trying to be upbeat, but it didn't sound like he believed it. "Coast still clear?" he asked Silas, who was back at his post, standing on a desk so he could see out the window.

Silas shrugged. "I think so. Then again, it's so dark out, I can barely see two feet in front of my face."

"Very comforting," Nick muttered.

"Yes," Tesla said firmly. "It is."

Nick sighed and then nodded. This "being positive" stuff was harder than he thought. But he understood Tesla's point. For what they planned next, the darker the better.

"All right," Nick said. "Let's see who the lucky one is."

He held out a fist. Tesla and DeMarco followed suit.

"One," said Nick, pumping his fist up and down. The others did likewise. "Two. *Three*."

Two of the hands stayed balled into fists. The third flattened out, palm down.

Two rocks, one paper.

Two losers, one winner.

"Dang," said DeMarco.

"Darn," said Tesla.

"Woo-hoo," said Nick—the one who'd chosen paper—unenthusiastically.

"Best two out of three?" DeMarco suggested.

Nick shook his head and bent down to pick up the rover.

They'd only been able to get a window open far enough for someone small—that is, anyone but Silas—to slip through. Nick had just won the honor. Now it would be his job to take the rover out to the road and position it to drive away once the rising sun began to power it.

Nick climbed onto a desk and stared at the open window, unsure of the best way to get out. After a moment or two, he decided that headfirst made the most sense. He bent over and started trying to snake his way through the opening.

"Let me help," Silas said behind him.

Nick was about to tell him not to bother—"Let me help" were ominous words coming from Silas—but before he could speak, he felt hands grasp his ankles and jerk his feet off the floor.

"Whoa, whoa, whoa!" Nick cried as he shot outside. He ended up in a heap on the cool, hard pavement by the side of the building.

"Geez, guys," he heard Tesla say. "Ever hear of being sneaky?"

Nick wanted to zing his sister with a snappy

comeback, but he couldn't think of one. Getting shoved through an open window can rattle a guy.

He stood and dusted himself off, then stepped back to the window. Tesla was waiting with the rover, which she carefully maneuvered past the glass and into Nick's waiting hands.

"Julie or the old ladies could come back any second to check on us," Tesla said. "Don't take any longer than you have to."

"That was my plan, Tez," Nick said.

"And be careful," Tesla added.

"That was my plan, too." Nick turned and walked away.

Tesla stuck her head out the window to watch him go. It was no use, though. The night was utterly dark, and after only a few steps he disappeared into blackness.

Nick knew he was walking along the side of the building—he could see it as a ghostly gray blob to his left—but he couldn't make out any other part of the abandoned base. He looked up, searching the sky for the moon. It wasn't there. Still, he stopped to stare in wonderment at what he *did* see.

Ablaze above him were countless stars, the core of the Milky Way cutting across them in a long, cloudy, diagonal ripple. It was the most beautiful, brilliant nighttime sky Nick had ever seen.

Nick could feel a chilly wind blowing over the desert. The paper they had taped to the side of the solar rover fluttered in the breeze.

Written on the paper was this:

HELP! WE ARE BEING
HELD PRISONER AT BRACE
AIR FORCE BASE. PLEASE
CONTACT THE FBI AND
HAVE THEM ALERT "AGENT
McINTYRE" IMMEDIATELY!

Sorry we don't know her first name

Nick Holt
Tesla Holt
DeMarco Davison
Silas Kuskie

The fate of the free world may depend on it!

Most of the note had been written by Tesla, because the boys assumed she'd have the best handwriting. ("That's sexist," Tesla had complained at first. She stopped arguing after the guys showed her what their penmanship looked like.)

The "Sorry—we don't know her first name" part had been added by Nick, who was worried the note wasn't specific enough.

The "The fate of the free world may depend on it!" part had been added by DeMarco, who was worried the note wasn't dramatic enough.

Silas wanted to add illustrations, because he was worried the note wasn't visual enough, but the others told him that was unnecessary. (They also knew that a condor would end up in the drawings, and that would just confuse people.)

Nick nervously ran a thumb over the tape fastening the note to the rover. It would have to hold as the little makeshift car rolled its way over dozens of miles of dusty road. If it didn't, the note—and their only hope of rescue—would drop off and flutter away into the sun-baked desert bleakness. Never to be seen again.

Like them, perhaps.

The muddled gray blob beside Nick—the wall he'd been walking beside—suddenly disappeared. He'd reached the end of the building and kept walking without even realizing it. He was out in the open now. And the moonlight, faint as it was, made Nick feel like he was standing in a spotlight.

Nick quickly backed up until he was hidden again by the building. Then slowly, cautiously, he peeped around the corner. A crescent moon hung low in the sky. It gave just enough light to create recognizable silhouettes. Nick could make out more buildings, a hangar, the truck that had brought them all there.

But no people. At least not out in the open. If anyone was around, they were sticking to the shadows.

Nick did the same as he eased around the building and began creeping toward the long, unwinding road that stretched off to the horizon on the other side of the truck. Eventually, he again had to step out into the open and leave the building—and the cover it provided—behind.

Once he was in the moonlight, plainly visible to anyone who might happen to look his way, Nick wasn't sure which was the better option: Should he move slowly but quietly? Or fast but not so quietly?

Nick opted for slow but quiet. His decision wasn't made so much because he didn't want anyone to hear him. He just couldn't stand the thought that someone else might be out there, someone *he* couldn't hear. So Nick took steady, near-silent steps until he reached the road, his eyes scanning the black void on either side of him, his ears straining to pick up the slightest sign that he wasn't alone. Then he walked along the roadside with no specific destination in mind beyond *far enough*. He couldn't take the chance that Bob or one of his flunkies would spot the rover in the morning. Nick had to give their vehicle as big a head start as possible.

This will do, one part of Nick's psyche said after he'd been walking along the road for a minute or two.

No, it won't, said another, braver part.

Nick continued walking for about another minute. Then he froze.

A soft, swishing sound raised goosebumps on the back of his neck. The noise wasn't coming from behind him, from the base. It was off to his right somewhere.

It was coming from the desert!

Nick heard it again. A sort of shushing. *Sh-sh-sh-sh-sh . . .*

He realized it was the sound of light, fast footsteps in sand. And they were coming closer.

Told you! said the first part of Nick.

Shut up, said the second.

Will you just put down the darned car and run away already? said a third.

"Good idea," Nick muttered to himself. He squatted and carefully positioned the rover so that it was perfectly straight on the road, as straight as he could orient it in the faint moonlight. Then he stood up, spun around, and started running.

Had the shushing footsteps stopped? Nick couldn't hear anything except for his own panting and his footsteps slapping hard on the pavement. He thought he saw something out of the corner of his eye but couldn't be sure.

Low, shifting shadows by the side of the road . . . no, by the *sides* of the road. They were on both sides of him. Whoever or whatever "they" were.

Nick started running faster—faster than he had ever run in his life. But it wasn't fast enough.

The shapes stayed with him, ever so close

behind. However, the sound they made changed. Instead of *sh-sh-sh-sh*, Nick now heard *clack-clack-clack-clack*. Nick was certain he was hearing claws running on blacktop. The things from the desert—the shadows—were on the road with him. And they were closing in fast!

Nick opened his mouth not knowing if he was about to shout for help or scream bloody murder.

It didn't matter. All he managed to say was "Oof!" He'd run straight into something *else* in the dark—something that crashed to the asphalt with him and said "Oof!" too.

"Go! Get out of here, you mutts!" a familiar voice shouted nearby. "I might look small, but I'm tough!"

"DeMarco?" said Nick. He blinked at the person he'd just accidentally tackled. "Tez?"

"I don't think we want to be lying on the ground just now, Nick," Tesla said.

"Oh. Right!"

Nick hopped up, and his sister did the same. They turned to find DeMarco stamping his feet and waving his arms at two snarling, glowering, doglike animals.

They weren't dogs, though. They were either small wolves or large coyotes.

Nick and Tesla started stamping their feet and waving their arms, too.

With a lip-curling snap, one of the animals wheeled around and skulked away into the desert. The other watched the kids for another moment, then slowly turned and casually trotted off up the road. Nick could still hear the *clack-clack-clack* of its claws long after it was gone from sight.

Nick let out a sigh of relief. "Thanks, guys. How did you know those things were out here?"

"We didn't," said Tesla. "We just wanted to see

what was taking you so long."

"We'd better get back fast," said DeMarco, peering toward the base. "It doesn't look like anyone heard us, but the longer we're gone, the greater the chance someone will notice."

Nick didn't argue. He disliked being a prisoner, but at that particular moment it sure beat walking around free in a coyote-filled desert.

As the kids hustled back onto the base, they heard a yipping cry in the darkness behind them. It was answered by another howl off to their left. Then another to the right.

No wonder Bob hadn't bothered stationing Ethel or Gladys or Julie as guards outside. The desert was full of watchful eyes already. His captives weren't going anywhere.

Until the sun came up, that is.

If they were lucky.

First it was discomfort that kept Nick awake. All the kids had to sleep on were the scruffy old sofa cushions Ethel (or Gladys) had given them, and they were so thin that it was impossible to get comfortable on the room's cold, hard tile floor.

As the night wore on, then it was hunger and thirst that kept Nick awake. After divvying up the stale tortilla chips Gladys (or Ethel) had brought them for dinner, each of the kids received exactly seven and a half chips—and no water to wash them down.

Eventually, dawn came, and sunlight streamed through their room's small window. But it wasn't the harsh, unfiltered light of the desert morning that kept Nick from finally nodding off. Now it was worry.

"Hey, Tez . . . you awake?" Nick whispered.

"I am now," Tesla said.

"I was never asleep," said Silas.

"Me, neither," said DeMarco. "It's been a *long* night."

"I know what you mean," said Nick. "How far do you think the rover's gone by now, Tez?"

Tesla shrugged without opening her eyes. "I don't know. Maybe a quarter of a mile."

"That's not far," said Nick.

"Not far? It's *nothing*," said DeMarco.

"Patience, guys, patience," said Tesla.

She rolled onto her side and began breathing deeply in a way that almost sounded like a snore. But Nick wasn't fooled.

He finally gave up on sleep entirely and got up, walking over to the window. He stood there for a long, long time, one ear cocked to catch the sound of approaching sirens or helicopters or tanks or *any-thing*. But all he heard were the other kids either trying to sleep or pretending to.

Soon DeMarco got up and joined him. A minute later, Silas did the same.

"Hear anything?" Silas asked.

"No," Nick and DeMarco said together.

"Patience, guys," said Tesla through a huge yawn. "Patience."

She reached over, picked up the cushion on which Nick had tossed and turned all night, and put it over her head.

"You're not fooling anyone," said Nick. "You're as awake and as worried as we are."

"Zzzzzzz," came Tesla's reply.

Of course, you can lie on the floor with a sofa cushion over your head for only so long, even when you're trying to be the model of nonchalant calm. So eventually Tesla got up and joined the boys by the window.

She gazed up at the sky, then down at the shadows stretching out from the side of the building.

"It must be at least nine o'clock," she said. "I bet

the rover's gone a mile by now."

"How far does it need to go?" Silas asked.

A lot more than a mile, Nick almost answered. But he stayed silent. He was still trying to be more upbeat, after all. "Who knows?" he said instead. Which wasn't exactly upbeat but wasn't necessarily downbeat, either.

"I bet it's a lot more than a mile," DeMarco muttered.

Boy, Nick thought, *he's been hanging out with me too much.*

"I keep telling you guys to chill out," Tesla said. "We've sent for help. All we have to worry about now is trying not to die of boredom while we wait for it to arrive."

Suddenly, they heard a squealing gurgle, and an embarrassed Silas slapped his hands over his belly. "And starving," he said.

"Hey," said DeMarco, turning toward the door. All the other kids heard the noise, too: footsteps in the hallway. The door swung open, too quickly for them to stash anything . . . though fortunately, with the rover out on the road, they no longer had anything they needed to hide.

NICK AND TESLA'S SOLAR-POWERED SHOWDOWN

"Good morning!" Tesla said cheerfully.

Julie Casserly smirked back from the doorway, with an equally smirky Ethel and Gladys right behind her. "Bob's throwing a pizza party," Julie said. She swept out her arm, inviting the kids to join her in the hall. "And you're invited."

"Pizza party? Woo-hoo!" said Silas. "Guess we won't be starving!"

"Or dying of boredom," said DeMarco.

The two boys left the room, followed by Tesla. Nick was the last to go. The women's sneering grins sent a chill down his spine.

If they've got reason to smile, the not-so-upbeat part of Nick couldn't help thinking, *we've got reason to frown . . .*

Julie led the way through the building while Ethel and Gladys brought up the rear, making sure the kids followed. The hallways looked familiar, and it soon became clear why.

Bob's "pizza party" was taking place in the same musty old control room where they'd met him the day before. When Julie led her prisoners inside, they found Bob already there, along with Mr. and Mrs. Holt, Uncle Newt, and a tall, lean, gray-haired man in a black suit. Agent Doyle.

"Hello, children," Agent Doyle said with a smile.

None of the kids smiled back. They just stared (or, in the case of Nick and Tesla, glared) back at him.

"Now, now. Don't be like that to good ol' Doyle," Bob admonished them. He was wearing a different Hawaiian shirt—this one had parrots and palm trees printed on it. "He brought the pizza!"

Bob waved a hand at a flat, square box sitting atop one of the workstations nearby. Printed on the top flap was a cartoon of a stout, mustachioed chef taking a pizza out of an oven.

"Sorry, guys—I'm hungry," Silas said as he rushed toward the box. He flipped up the lid, revealing a half-eaten pepperoni and black olive pizza beneath. Silas pulled off a slice and stuffed two-thirds of it into his mouth.

"You should *all* eat," said Nick and Tesla's father, "before Bob changes his mind and—"

"Tut-tut, Albert!" Bob snapped. "I told you once already: this is my pizza party with my rules. You three will keep your mouths *closed* . . . except to eat pizza."

"Oh, shut up, Bob," Mrs. Holt shot back.

She and her husband were sitting at one of the workstations in the corner, with Uncle Newt standing beside them.

Mrs. Holt stood and walked toward the kids.

"Sit down, Martha," Bob said.

Mrs. Holt hugged Nick and Tesla and kissed the tops of their heads.

Nick hugged her back.

"Geez, Mom," Tesla protested under her breath. "Not in front of the bad guys."

"Sit down, Martha," Bob repeated more harshly.

"You've kept us from our children for weeks," Mr. Holt snapped at him. "The least you can do is let their mother say good morning."

Bob's face began to turn pepperoni-red.

"My pizza party, my rules!" he barked. "Now get back to your seat before I put you there by force!"

Mrs. Holt shot her former boss a withering look. But after giving Nick and Tesla another quick hug, she did as she was told.

Uncle Newt glowered at Bob as Martha Holt

returned to her workstation. Tesla had never seen her uncle look as if he wanted to punch someone, but he sure looked like he wanted to take a swing at Bob.

If Bob noticed, he didn't care. He turned and flashed a grin at Nick and Tesla and DeMarco, the color already leaving his cheeks.

"Please," he said, gesturing again at the pizza, "help yourselves."

When the kids didn't move immediately, the sentiment behind his smile soured and his expression turned scornful.

"You do not want to ruin my pizza party," Bob hissed at them.

"Come on, guys," Tesla said, starting toward the pizza.

"Some party," DeMarco muttered as he followed her.

Silas was already starting on his second slice when the other kids joined him. Tesla picked up a piece, even though Bob's insanity had ruined her appetite. She wasn't interested in eating any pizza. But she did want to judge how old it was.

If Agent Doyle had arrived the night before, he

might have driven up to the base before Nick snuck outside. Which would mean the solar-powered car was safe. And even if he had shown up after Nick went out to the road, he might not have noticed the rover in the dark. But if he'd just arrived at the base that morning, in the full light of day, there was no way he could have missed it.

Tesla took a bite of the pizza. It was room temperature. The crust was hard, the cheese ungooey, the sauce congealed.

This pizza was not fresh.

Tesla considered this data point furiously. It was midmorning, and they were in the middle of nowhere. It's not like an open Domino's was right across the road. The pizza was bound to be old and stale.

But how old was it? Late last night old? Early this morning old? When and where had Agent Doyle bought it? And when did he bring it to—?

Tesla froze midthought. Midchew, even. For a long moment she stood there, her mouth full of half-chewed stale pizza, staring at a TV screen that had caught her attention.

Nick noticed and followed his sister's gaze.

"What's the matter, Tez?" he whispered. "Is something—oh."

He didn't even bother finishing his question. He didn't need to. Nick recognized what was on the monitor, and it gave him his answer:

A small, dark, boxy object was moving along a gray strip that cut through a sparse yellow landscape. The image was taken from above, as if the camera were high up in a hot-air balloon.

Or a satellite.

Nick and Tesla were looking down on their solar rover as it rolled slowly and steadily along the road.

"Amazing picture, isn't it?" said Bob, beaming with pride. "The satellite's a hundred and fifty miles above us, and still it could find your little contraption practically the moment the sun came up."

Silas and DeMarco looked up from eating. "What's he talking about?" DeMarco asked.

Nick pointed at the monitor on the other side of the room. "The solar rover," he said. "They know about it."

"Know about it?" Bob chuckled. "I *wanted* you to build it! We've dealt with you kids before, remember? I know how good you are with gadgets. So I made sure we left you exactly what you'd need to whip up some kind of solar-powered model car."

Tesla was tempted to spit out the chewy, tasteless pizza, but she forced herself to swallow it instead. "Why?" she asked, tossing the rest of her slice back into the box.

"Target practice!" Bob said gleefully. He turned to Mr. and Mrs. Holt and Uncle Newt. "The satellite's locked on," he told them. "Show me what it can do . . . or I'll have Agent Doyle take four new targets into the desert."

Just in case they didn't understand what he was implying, Bob jerked his head at the kids.

Mr. and Mrs. Holt looked at each other and then at Uncle Newt. They didn't speak or nod or shrug or shake their heads. Everything they needed to say to each other was communicated by the haunted, trapped looks on their faces. Then each of the three scientists turned to the nearest control panels and began pressing buttons and typing instructions.

"Hoo, boy! Here we go!" Bob said. He clapped his hands and bounced on the balls of his feet, giggling with delight. "Finally, finally, finally!"

Nick and Tesla also shared a silent look, as their

parents and uncle had. Only theirs communicated one thing: *this guy is nuts*.

"Keep your eyes on the screen, everybody!" Bob said. "This is a historic moment!" And then his enthusiasm dimmed a tiny bit. "Or should that be *an* historic moment?" he mused. "Oh, well, whatever. This is big!"

Bob went back to bouncing and clapping. For a while. But when half a minute passed and nothing changed on the screen, his bounces grew less bouncy, and his clapping all but stopped.

"Where is it?" he said. "Where is my outer-space death ray?"

Uncle Newt looked up from his keyboard to scowl at the man contemptuously. "It's there," he said. "Microwaves are invisible, remember?"

"But I don't see any . . . a-ha!"

Bob began bouncing and clapping again.

Tufts of smoke were beginning to trail away from the boxy object at the center of the monitor screen. The smoke started off wispy and gray but grew thicker and darker with each passing second.

Then the smoke stopped. And so did the rover.

"Is that it?" Julie asked. "Isn't it going to explode?"

"Why would it explode?" asked Uncle Newt.

Julie flapped a hand at the screen. "You know . . . outer-space death ray."

Mrs. Holt shook her head and sighed. "It's not an outer-space death ray. It's just a power transmitter."

"I beg to differ, Doctor!" Bob trilled in a singsongy tone. He looked as if he was about to jump up and click his heels. "That gadget your kids built is most definitely dead . . . and you killed it. Congratulations!"

Uncle Newt and Mr. and Mrs. Holt looked thoroughly miserable.

"Now it's time to get ready for our first *real* target," Bob continued.

He walked over to the wall of blank TV screens and turned one on. It was the one that had been tuned to the cable news channel the day before. The news channel came back on. The sound was muted, but it was obvious that the reporters were still talking about the same topic.

A woman was waving to a crowd as she stepped out of a limousine. Under her were the words DIGNITARIES ARRIVE FOR "STAR WARS" SUMMIT.

"The weakling-in-chief is going to be signing the

227

space weapons ban tomorrow in the White House Rose Garden at nine-thirty a.m. Eastern Time," Bob said. "And that's when we'll show the world what happens to anyone who sells out or threatens the U. S. of A."

"What are you saying?" DeMarco asked. "You're gonna fry the president?"

Bob shook his head. "Oh, no, no, no, no, no. Haven't you been paying attention? We're not going to fry the president. We'd need hot oil for that. We're going to *microwave* the president. Like a bag of popcorn. And then we're going to microwave even more people!"

Agent Doyle and Julie Casserly noticed the looks of horror that the Holts and Uncle Newt and the kids were giving Bob.

"Only bad people, of course," said Agent Doyle.

"Bob's been working on a list," said Julie Casserly.

Bob smiled. "It's getting pretty long."

"Haven't you ever seen a James Bond movie?" Silas said to Bob. "News flash, dude: You're not the good guy. You're the crazy villain."

"You know what? I *love* James Bond movies," Bob said. "And I happen to think 007 would be on our side." Bob walked over to the pizza box and picked up a slice. With one hand, he brought it to his mouth to take a big bite. With the other, he slammed the box closed.

"Pizza party's over," he announced as he chewed. "Julie, take our little friends back to their playroom. We'll need them up before the sun tomorrow so that Dr. Holt, Dr. Holt, and Dr. Holt are all properly motivated to do as they're told."

He whirled toward Nick and Tesla's parents and their uncle.

"And no tearful farewells! No kisses! No hugs!" he said. "You'll have plenty of time for that once the Rose Garden is a smoking hole!"

"All right, boys and girl," Julie said to the kids. She'd been standing in the doorway, but now she stepped aside and gestured toward the hallway beyond. "Let's go."

"See you tomorrow!" Agent Doyle called out cheerfully, in a way that made Tesla want to kick him in the shin.

As they filed out of the room, both Nick and Tesla kept their eyes on their parents and Uncle Newt. They were looking for a signal, a sign, a reason to

229

hope. Their mother mouthing "We have a plan," maybe. Or their uncle blinking out THE ESCAPE IS AT MIDNIGHT in Morse code. Or even their father simply giving them a "Don't worry" wink.

Yet the adults just stared back at them silently, their eyes full of fear.

If Nick and Tesla wanted a reason to hope, it seemed they'd have to find it themselves.

"Do you really think that Bob guy makes any sense?" DeMarco asked Julie as she marched the kids down the hall. "The president won't let you use the satellite as a weapon, so you'll use it as a weapon on the president?"

"Bob is a great man," Julie said, staring straight ahead.

"Seems kind of traitor-y to me," Silas grumbled.

DeMarco looked over his shoulder at Ethel and Gladys. "How about you two? You don't think Bob's cuckoo bananas?"

They ignored him, so DeMarco turned back to Julie.

"What about that list of 'bad people' Bob's working on? Who's gonna be on it?" he said. "Can you really trust someone who gets *that* excited about having his own quote-unquote outer-space death ray?"

"Bob is a great man," Julie repeated robotically.

"You keep saying that. But he doesn't look so great to me," DeMarco said. "I mean, do great men wear Hawaiian shirts?"

Julie finally looked at DeMarco, her brow furrowed. She seemed to be considering his question.

She thought for a long moment before giving him her answer.

"Shut up, kid."

"Here again," Silas said once Julie and the old ladies locked them back into the junk-filled office they'd spent the night in. "And I'm still hungry."

"We don't have to be here for long," said DeMarco. "As soon as it's dark, we can make a break for it."

Silas pointed to the windows along the far wall.

"You can, maybe. But I'm too big to get out that

way." he said. "And anyway, where would we go? We're still in the middle of a desert."

DeMarco crossed his arms over his chest. "Better to die of thirst or be torn apart by coyotes than stay here and . . ." His voice trailed off as his own words sank in. Then he slumped down onto a cushion on the floor. "You're right," he groaned. "We're not going anywhere."

"We wouldn't run away even if we could," Nick said.

DeMarco and Silas gaped at him in surprise.

"We wouldn't?" Silas said.

Nick shook his head.

"You heard Bob," said Tesla. "He wants to pop the president of the United States like a bag of popcorn."

"We can't let that happen," said Nick. For once it was easy for him to sound as resolute as his sister.

Tesla noticed the change in Nick. She glanced over and gave him a quick but approving grin.

"Guys," said DeMarco, "we've stopped, like, crooks and thieves and idiots trying to ruin a movie. This is out of our league. Like Silas said to Bob: this is James Bond stuff."

"Well, how does James Bond always save the

day?" Nick asked.

"Ooo! Ooo! I know!" Silas said, raising his hand. "He blows up the bad guys' hideout!"

"Which we are currently *in*," DeMarco said

"That wasn't what I was thinking," said Nick.

Tesla pointed at a pile of electronic equipment on one of the desks. "Nick's talking about gadgets," she said. "And they've left us enough stuff to build one more."

She began pacing in a slow circle, scanning the room. Nick did the same.

When they stopped, they were both pointed in the same direction: toward the door.

"A-ha," said Nick.

"Exactly," said Tesla.

"We're gonna make a gadget out of a door?" said DeMarco.

"Look *over* the door," said Nick.

"Ohhhhhhh," said Silas and DeMarco.

Jutting out from the wall above the door was a metallic-gray dome about the size of a cereal bowl.

An alarm bell.

Nick and Tesla looked at each other and nodded. They'd found their hope.

SUN-ACTIVATED ALARM CLOCK/ VILLAIN DISTRACTOR

THE STUFF

- A hotel bell (available at office supply stores) or bicycle bell

- A mini vibration motor

- A small nut

- Brass brads

- A paper clip

- A metal coat hanger

- Thin plastic-coated wire

- Electrical tape

- Cardboard

- A solar panel that can output 3 or 4.5 volts

- A wire cutter

- A hot-glue gun

- Pliers

THE SETUP

1. Very carefully, trim some of the plastic off the ends of the motor wires, leaving about ½ inch (1.25 cm) of wire exposed. Hot-glue the wires at the base of the motor (so they won't break when the motor is hanging).

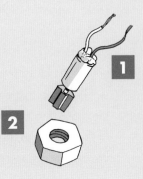

2. Check that the nut just fits over the spinning part of the motor. Slip it into place, making sure the motor can still spin, and then dab a little glue to secure it.

3. Use wire clippers to cut a length of wire from the coat hanger; about 20 inches (51 cm) should be enough. Bend one end of the coat hanger wire to fit around the base of the bell and glue it in place. Bend the rest of the wire at a 90-degree angle so it reaches over the bell, as shown.

4. Hot-glue the motor wires to the end of the coat hanger; glue them near the middle of the wires so that the motor hangs down with the nut barely touching the bell. Place the glue somewhere in the middle of the two

wires, then bend the coat hanger up or down as needed so that the nut is at the right height.

5. Next, make a switch (unless you want your alarm to ring continuously whenever the solar panel is in the sun). Slip one of the brads through one end of the paper clip, then pin the clip flat against the

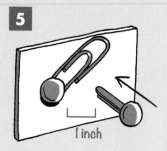

cardboard. Pin the other brad through the cardboard, positioned about 1 inch (2.5 cm) from the other brad, so the paper clip can be moved to touch the second brad.

THE FINAL STEPS

1. Wire the switch: Cut two lengths of wire about 1 foot (30.5 cm) long, or longer if you want your alarm to be farther from the sunlight. Cut one of the wires in half. Carefully trim back the plastic coating on all ends.

2. Connect one of the two shorter wires to each of the brads, twisting them tightly around the brads to create a good connection. Hot-glue the longer piece of wire in place on the cardboard, lengthwise, with the ends running off the cardboard. You should have a pair of free wires extending from each end of the cardboard.

3. Connect the wires from one end of the cardboard to the wires coming out of the motor. Connect the wires from the other side of the cardboard to the wires coming out of the solar panel. Wrap electrical tape around all the connections.

4. To operate your alarm/distractor, place the solar panel in bright, direct sunlight. Turn on the switch by moving the paper clip to connect the two brads. Or leave the alarm where sunlight will hit the solar panel at the time you want. When the sun reaches the panel, the alarm will sound.

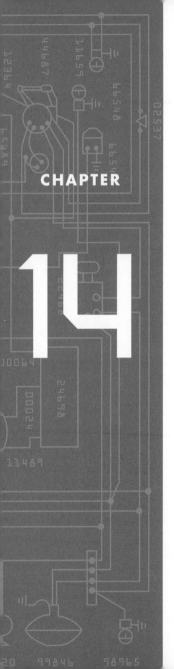

The sun hadn't yet risen the next morning when Julie and Ethel and Gladys came to wake up the kids.

"Come on, get up," Julie said after flicking on the overhead lights. "It's showtime."

Nick, Tesla, Silas, and DeMarco rose groggily from their cushions and started trudging toward the door. Nick couldn't resist the urge to sneak a peek back at the windows as they went.

Was that a glimmer of dawn's light in the far left corner? Maybe. But Nick didn't let himself look long enough to be sure. He didn't want

Julie or the old ladies following his gaze and noticing what was in the far *right* corner: the wire running out to the solar panel they'd propped against the side of the building.

"Will there be pizza?" Silas asked while being escorted through the halls.

The women ignored him.

"This is your last chance," DeMarco said to Julie. "You can still help us stop Bob before you commit treason."

Julie stayed silent and smirked at him before looking away. She began whistling "Hail to the Chief."

A moment later, the group was walking into the control room. Nick and Tesla's parents and Uncle Newt were still hunched over the same workstation they'd been at the day before. To judge by the bags under their eyes and the haggard expressions, they'd been there all night.

Bob and Agent Doyle, by contrast, looked rested and refreshed. Bob was in yet another Hawaiian shirt, this one featuring a kaleidoscopic potpourri of pineapples, coconuts, bananas, and butterflies. Agent Doyle had traded in his usual black suit for a colorful Hawaiian shirt of his own. He seemed to be in a festive mood.

"And here they are! Our insurance policy," Agent Doyle said with a grin as the kids entered the room. He turned toward Mr. and Mrs. Holt and Uncle Newt. "Just remember who's next on Bob's Zap List if you don't follow orders."

The adults glared at him but said nothing.

Mr. Holt gave the kids a silent wave. Mrs. Holt smiled at them in a tired, sad, trying-to-be-reassuring-and-failing sort of way. Uncle Newt just kept scowling at Agent Doyle and Bob, his fists clenched tight.

"That's quite a shirt, Agent Doyle," DeMarco said. "Reminds me of the time I went on a rollercoaster after eating two corn dogs and an extra-large slush-ie." DeMarco clutched his stomach and pretended to vomit.

"Hey, you're right!" said Silas, pointing at the shirt. "Same splash pattern!"

Agent Doyle didn't let the insult bother him.

"I'm not 'Agent' Doyle anymore. As of yesterday, I'm officially retired," he said genially. "No more suits for me. Now I can serve my country in style."

"I don't think you and I have the same definition

of 'style,' *Mr.* Doyle," said DeMarco.

"Or serving our country," Nick added.

"Ironic, isn't it?" Tesla said. "About to stab their country in the back, and they dress like they're going to a Fourth of July barbecue."

"Yeah," said Silas. "It's as if Arnold Benedict sold us out to the Germans in his pajamas."

The other kids looked at Silas confusedly. The plan had been to distract and delay Bob and his gang by drawing them into an argument, not pelting them with non sequiturs.

Silas winked and gave his friends a (he seemed to think) surreptitious thumbs-up. Apparently, he really didn't know that it was *Benedict Arnold* who betrayed America to the *English*. "And another thing . . ." he said.

Bob shushed him without even bothering to look up. "Quiet!" he said. "It's about to begin."

He was staring at the TV tuned to the cable news station. On the screen, the president was stepping up to a podium in the White House Rose Garden while a bunch of other serious-looking adults in suits stood around watching.

"Good morning," the president said. "We are

gathered here today for a historic moment."

"So it is *a* historic," Bob said. "Well, however you say it, the president's right—only we're the ones who are going to be making the history!"

He snapped his fingers at Nick and Tesla's parents and uncle.

"I want the satellite view. *Now.*"

"It's already up," said Mrs. Holt.

"What? Where?"

Mr. Holt pointed to a nearby monitor. "There."

Everyone turned toward the screen he'd indicated. It seemed to be broken; all that showed was a wall of white with the occasional gray streak or swirl floating through it.

"Where's the White House?" Doyle asked.

"Under that," said Mrs. Holt. "Those are clouds."

"*What?*" Bob barked impatiently.

"It's overcast in Washington this morning," Uncle Newt explained. "We don't control the weather."

Doyle moved across the room to stand behind the kids. "Well, you'd better find a way to see through those clouds," he growled. "And fast!"

As Uncle Newt and Mr. and Mrs. Holt got back to work, pushing buttons and fiddling with knobs, Nick gave his sister a nudge. When she peeked his way, he widened his eyes. *Is that alarm of ours* ever *going to go off?* his expression said.

Tesla answered with a tiny shrug.

But her brain was spinning furiously. Their parents' work was about to be turned into a dreadful weapon. The president of the United States was in mortal danger. *They* were in mortal danger. And the one thing that might make the difference between success and disaster, victory and defeat, life and death, was a gizmo she and her brother and friends had cobbled together out of scraps and trash.

Tesla used to think that competing in a science fair was a lot of pressure. But the worst that could happen at one was not winning first place. The worst that might happen right *now* was . . .

Tesla didn't let herself think about it.

"There! That's doing it!" Bob said. He was leaning so close to the monitor of the satellite view that his nose was practically touching the screen. "I'm starting to see something through the clouds!"

The sound of polite applause was coming from the news broadcast. "The president's done talking. They're about to sign the treaty," said Doyle impatiently.

Doyle laid a heavy hand on Tesla's shoulder. A part of her wanted to shudder. Another wanted to grab the hand and bite it as hard as she could. Somehow she managed to resist both impulses. For now.

"Lock onto our target *immediately*," Doyle snapped, "or the girl's going to be the first one we take outside and—"

BRRRRRRRRRRRRRRRRRRRRRRINNNNNNNNNNNNG!

"What's that?" Bob said, whirling away from the monitor.

At last, the alarm bell was doing its thing!

Julie stepped into the hall with Ethel and Gladys. "It's coming from that way," she said, pointing. "From the room where we've been keeping the kids."

"Do you think the smoke detectors in this place could still be working?" Doyle asked Bob.

Bob's face went pale.

Tesla crossed her arms and tried to look smug. They hadn't started a fire, of course, but it couldn't hurt to act as if they had.

"A fire could force us out of the building or take out the power. It could ruin everything!" Bob said. He turned to Julie and the old ladies. "Get back to that room and find out what's going on!"

"Right!" Julie said. "Come on!"

The three women dashed up the hallway.

Doyle's grip on Tesla's shoulder tightened.

"What are you brats trying to pull?" he demanded.

"Should we show him?" Nick asked Silas and De-Marco.

The two boys nodded—then spun around and bolted for the door.

Before Doyle could react, two things happened: Nick stomped on his foot . . . and Tesla stopped resisting the temptation to bite his fingers.

As Doyle howled in pain, Silas and DeMarco slammed the control-room door shut and started searching for the lock.

"You little idiots!" Bob bellowed, stepping toward the boys. "Get away from there!"

He felt a little tap on his shoulder.

Bob turned to see who it was.

That's when Uncle Newt punched him squarely in the nose.

"Oof!" said Bob, his head snapping back.

"Ow!" said Uncle Newt, shaking his hand. He couldn't help but make a mental note of his new

245

discovery: punching people *hurts*.

"We can't lock the door!" DeMarco cried. "You need a key!"

Half of their plan went out the window. The whole point had been to lure as many bad guys as possible out of the control room and lock the door behind them. Then . . . well, the kids weren't really sure what they were going to do after that, but at least they could delay the action until the president was safe. Especially with their parents and uncle there to help. But if Julie and Ethel and Gladys could get back inside the control room . . . it would all be for nothing.

"Maramay muh mooah!" Tesla said.

"What?" said Silas.

"*Maramay muh mooah!*"

Tesla couldn't enunciate any better than that because her teeth were still clamped down on Doyle's index, middle, and ring fingers. Doyle had fallen to his knees and was trying to push Tesla away, but Nick was hanging on to the man's free arm with all the strength he could muster. Nick understood what his sister was saying: "Barricade the door!" he translated while stomping on Doyle's other foot.

Silas and DeMarco turned and scanned the room frantically.

"With what?" DeMarco yelled.

The control room's computer workstations were attached to the floor and couldn't be moved. And all the chairs had wheels, so there was no way to wedge one under the door handle.

"There's only one thing we've got to keep those ladies out, dude," Silas said. He pressed a shoulder to the door and leaned against it hard. "Us."

DeMarco nodded, placed his hands against the door, and waited beside his friend for the push they both knew was coming.

"Activate the microwave beam!" Bob roared at Mr. and Mrs. Holt. He was staggering back from Uncle Newt, his hands pressed against his bloodied nose. "Now!"

Doyle finally managed to pry his hand from Tesla's mouth, and then he shoved both her and Nick away. He reflexively reached toward his left armpit . . . but grabbed only a bunch of colorful polyester. Because now that Agent Doyle was no longer an agent, what he usually kept tucked in a shoulder holster—his government-issued sidearm—was no longer there.

Apparently he'd switched from black suits to Hawaiian shirts a little too soon.

Doyle spat out a curse and then turned to face Mr. and Mrs. Holt. "Do as Bob says. Burn the White House," he said. "There's no escape for you. You're only delaying the inevitable."

Before either of the Holts could reply, Silas and DeMarco yelped in alarm.

They'd felt a push against the door.

Julie and Ethel and Gladys had figured out there was no fire. Now they were back—and they wanted in.

"What's going on in there?" Julie yelled from the hallway. "Let us in!"

"Not by the hairs of our chinny-chin-chins!" Silas called back.

The boys felt another push on the control room door—this time so hard that they were barely able to resist it. "Don't provoke them!" DeMarco told Silas.

"I think it's a little late to worry about that," Silas replied.

Bob and Doyle sprung into action and started moving toward the boys. Uncle Newt ran over to block them, and Nick and Tesla and their father scrambled over to line up alongside him. "Neither of you are threatening any children ever again," Mr. Holt said.

Mrs. Holt, meanwhile, hurried over to help Silas and DeMarco keep Julie and her flunkies out. She put her shoulder to the door just as another shove slammed against it—the strongest one yet—thrusting the boys back half a step.

"That wasn't just Julie," DeMarco said. "Ethel and Gladys are pushing, too."

Silas shivered. "Man, those old ladies creep me out."

Another push thrusted against the door came, opening it just wide and just long enough for Ethel (or Gladys) to snarl at Silas, "I heard that!"

Silas shivered again.

Bob and Doyle stood facing the resolute line of Nick and Tesla, their father, and their uncle. Bob still had his palms pressed to his injured nose. Doyle seemed unsure what to do next; he was a trained federal agent, but not only was he unarmed, his hand was also still throbbing. He could tell by the faces of the elder Holts—not to mention those of Nick and Tesla—that they weren't going to give up without a fight. Tesla opened her mouth and clacked her teeth together, causing Doyle to flinch.

"You can't keep my bodyguards out forever," Bob said, his voice muffled and guttural. He finally removed his hands from his face, revealing a nose that was swollen and red. "They're going to get back in."

"And when they do," continued Doyle, "someone's going to pay for this." He rubbed the fresh tooth marks on his left hand and glowered at Tesla. It was obvious who Doyle thought should pay first.

Suddenly, the sound of polite applause came from one of the televisions. The president was signing the treaty.

"At least we kept you from stopping this historic event," Tesla said.

Bob shrugged. "It won't matter in the long run. Or have you forgotten that I still have an outer-space death ray?"

"We keep telling you, Bob. It's not a death ray," said Mr. Holt. "And it never will be."

Bob smirked.

"Hey," said Silas, "where'd the ladies go? They're not pushing anymore."

"Somehow that makes me even more nervous," said DeMarco.

Mrs. Holt turned her head and pressed an ear to the door.

"I think I hear something," she said. "I don't know what they're up to out there, but we'd better get ready for—"

It was too late. They weren't ready.

Something slammed into the door with such force that it sent Silas, DeMarco, and Mrs. Holt flying backward.

Next, a whole swarm of people began streaming into the control room. But much to everyone's surprise, it wasn't Julie and the old ladies. It was a group of men wearing black jumpsuits and helmets. All but one were brandishing stubby assault rifles. The exception was the guy holding what looked like a large black pipe with red handles—the battering ram that had busted open the door.

"Go, go, go, go, go!" one of the men was yelling.

"Down, down, down, down, down!" screamed another.

"Hands up, up, up, up, up!" shouted a third.

Everyone but Silas dropped to the floor and put their hands up.

"Wait," said Silas. "Do you want us up or down?"

DeMarco pulled his friend to the floor.

Out in the hall, as DeMarco and Silas could now see, were Julie and Ethel and Gladys lying facedown with their hands cuffed behind their backs. "Are we being rescued or captured by somebody even worse?" said Silas.

"I have no idea," said DeMarco.

The men in black swept through the room, looking under and around every workstation and into every nook and cranny. Once it was obvious no one was hiding, they stopped, and one of them called out, "Clear!"

The announcement was followed by a second of silence and then a single sound: the *clack-clack-clack* of footsteps echoing down the hallway. The steps grew louder until a lone figure appeared in the doorway.

"All right, everybody—you can get up," said Agent McIntyre. "It's over."

The kids sprang to their feet wearing huge grins on their faces. The adults rose more slowly. And Bob and Doyle, who were surrounded by the black-garbed agents—they definitely *were not* smiling.

"How did you find us?" Nick asked.

Agent McIntyre held up a piece of singed, sun-faded paper.

> HELP! WE ARE BEING
> HELD PRISONER AT BRACE
> AIR FORCE BASE. PLEASE
> CONTACT THE FBI AND
> HAVE THEM ALERT "AGENT
> McINTYRE" IMMEDIATELY!
>
> Nick Holt
> Tesla Holt
> DeMarco Davison
> Silas Kuskie

Sorry we don't know her first name ←

The fate of the free world may depend on it!

"It's Gina, by the way," she said.

DeMarco cocked his head. "Huh? Who's Gina?"

Agent McIntyre pointed at herself. "I am. That's my first name."

"I can't believe our solar rover made it to the highway," Tesla said. "It looked like it was burned to a crisp."

"It *didn't* make it to the highway," said Agent McIntyre. "It was about half a mile up the access road, in the middle of nowhere."

"Then how did you find it?" asked Nick.

Uncle Newt walked back over to the computer station that he and Mr. and Mrs. Holt had been working at earlier, sporting a goofy grin on his face. "The government has lots of other satellites, you know," he said. "I'm assuming one of them spotted this."

When he typed a few lines of code into a keyboard, the picture on the nearest monitor began to change. The clouds it had been showing moved aside, for the first time revealing what was beneath them.

It wasn't Washington, D.C. It was a barren yellow landscape with a single black strip running through it.

They were looking down on the road leading to the base. A huge, black symbol and four words were burned into the desert soil to one side of the blacktop:

FOR GINA McINTYRE-FBI

The arrow was pointing to a gray smudge on the road: the melted remains of the solar rover.

"So the satellite was never over the White House?" Bob asked, incredulous. Both he and Doyle were now in handcuffs, held back by hulking federal agents gripping them by their elbows.

"Nope," Mrs. Holt said with obvious satisfaction. "The whole time we were pretending to adjust its position, we were really leaving that message in the desert."

"It was Newt's idea," said Mr. Holt, looking at his brother proudly.

Uncle Newt beamed at Nick and Tesla. "I've learned a thing or two this summer about improvising," he said.

"Ugh. Would you people just go ahead and do

a group hug so I can barf already?" grumbled ex-Agent Doyle.

Agent McIntyre looked at him, then at Bob, and shook her head sadly. "I am so disappointed in you two," she said. "Hawaiian shirts? Tacky."

"Are you almost done in there?" Ethel (or Gladys) called from the hallway. "I'm gettin' a little tired of lying here with my face on the floor."

"That group hug sounds like a good idea," said Tesla. "What do you say, guys?"

The Holts—Nick, Tesla, their parents, and their uncle—huddled up and threw their arms around one another. Rather than join in, Silas and DeMarco went around the room giving Agent McIntyre and the men in black high-fives.

The bad guys were defeated.

The good guys were reunited.

The world was safe.

And Nick and Tesla's summer vacation was finally over.

About the Authors

"SCIENCE BOB" PFLUGFELDER is an award-winning elementary school science teacher. His fun and informative approach to science has led to television appearances on the History Channel and *Access Hollywood*. He is also a regular guest on *Jimmy Kimmel Live*, *The Dr. Oz Show*, and *Live with Kelly & Michael*. Articles on Bob's experiments have appeared in *People*, *Nickelodeon* magazine, *Popular Science*, *Disney's Family Fun*, and *Wired*. He lives in Watertown, Massachusetts.

STEVE HOCKENSMITH is the author of the Edgar-nominated Holmes on the Range mystery series. His other books include the New York Times best seller *Pride and Prejudice and Zombies: Dawn of the Dreadfuls* and the short-story collection *Naughty: Nine Tales of Christmas Crime*. He lives with his wife and two children about forty minutes from Half Moon Bay, California.

NICK AND TESLA'S

SOLAR-POWERED LONG-RANGE
ROVER PROPELLER TEMPLATE

(see pages 194–200)

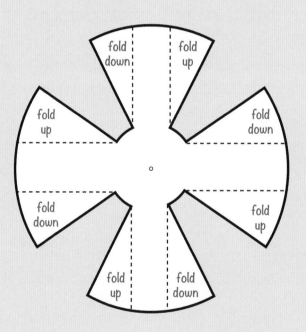

CATCH UP ON THE
NICK AND TESLA SERIES!

Nick and Tesla's
High-Voltage Danger Lab

Nick and Tesla's
Robot Army Rampage

Nick and Tesla's
Secret Agent Gadget Battle

Nick and Tesla's
Super-Cyborg Gadget Glove

Nick and Tesla's
Special Effects Spectacular

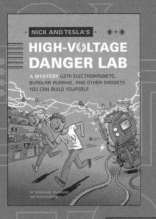

NICK AND TESLA'S

HIGH-VOLTAGE DANGER LAB

A MYSTERY WITH ELECTROMAGNETS, BURGLAR ALARMS, AND OTHER GADGETS YOU CAN BUILD YOURSELF

BY "SCIENCE BOB" PFLUGFELDER AND STEVE HOCKENSMITH

NICK AND TESLA'S

ROBOT ARMY RAMPAGE

A MYSTERY WITH HOVERBOTS, BRISTLEBOTS, AND OTHER ROBOTS YOU CAN BUILD YOURSELF

BY "SCIENCE BOB" PFLUGFELDER AND STEVE HOCKENSMITH

NICK AND TESLA'S

SECRET AGENT GADGET BATTLE

A MYSTERY WITH SPY CAMERAS, CODE WHEELS, AND OTHER GADGETS YOU CAN BUILD YOURSELF

BY "SCIENCE BOB" PFLUGFELDER AND STEVE HOCKENSMITH

NICK AND TESLA'S

SUPER-CYBORG GADGET GLOVE

A MYSTERY WITH A BLINKING, BEEPING, VOICE-RECORDING GADGET GLOVE YOU CAN BUILD YOURSELF

BY "SCIENCE BOB" PFLUGFELDER AND STEVE HOCKENSMITH

NICK AND TESLA'S

SPECIAL EFFECTS SPECTACULAR

A MYSTERY WITH ANIMATRONICS, ALIEN MAKEUP, CAMERA GEAR, AND OTHER MOVIE MAGIC YOU CAN MAKE YOURSELF

BY "SCIENCE BOB" PFLUGFELDER AND STEVE HOCKENSMITH

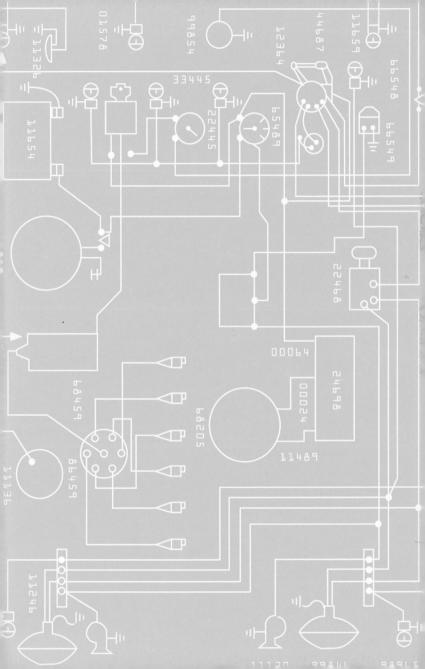

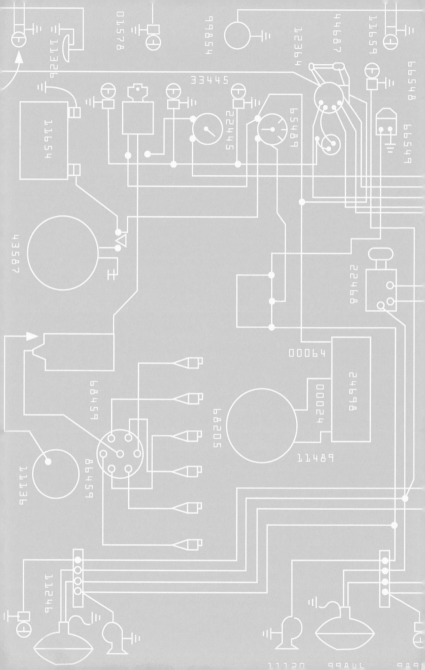